Dick Defenbach
1316 W. Olive St.

THE BOY SCOUT FIRE FIGHTERS

BY

IRVING CRUMP

Author of "Jack Straw in Mexico," "Jack
Straw, Lighthouse Builder," etc.

PUBLISHED WITH THE APPROVAL OF
THE BOY SCOUTS OF AMERICA

PUBLISHERS
BARSE & CO.
NEW YORK, N. Y.   NEWARK, N. J.

Printed in the United States of America

CONTENTS

THE BOY SCOUT FIRE FIGHTERS

CHAPTER I

THE MOTORCYCLE FIRE BRIGADE

"BY Jiminy, that was some fire for an old hay barn, wasn't it, fellows?" exclaimed Jiminy Gordon, as he entered the meeting room at headquarters. His eyes were flashing excitement and he was thoroughly out of breath from running up the long Otter Creek Hill. "I stayed until the last spark was out," he said, as he dropped into a chair beside Bruce Clifford, leader of the Owl Patrol of Quarry Troop No. 1.

"Some fire, is perfectly correct," said Bruce bitterly, "though it needn't have been anything more than an ordinary blaze. I tell you the Woodbridge Fire Department needs a little pep, fellows." This last was addressed to the four other occupants of the room, Bud Weir, Romper Ryan, Babe Wilson and Nipper Knapp.

"Right," said Romper.

"The way they went about it was a farce," said Bud.

"Yes, they all had to have their red flannel shirts on," remarked Babe, the fat boy, sarcastically.

"Say, did you see 'em scrapping over who should carry the fire trumpet?" laughed Romper.

"Sure, and about six men were giving orders," put in Jiminy, who had caught the spirit of the remarks.

"And no one obeyed any of 'em," supplemented Babe, sarcastic as usual.

"But the finest exhibition of firemanship was when one of the nozzlemen let go of the only hose they got on the fire while he hunted through his pockets for a paper of tobacco or something else just as important," said Bruce. "Of course the other nozzleman couldn't hold onto the hose alone and it twisted out of his hands. The thing acted like a big black snake, fellows, and hit Chief Blaney a whack in the chest that knocked him sprawling. Then it proceeded to wet down the whole fire department before some one captured it. It was a scream. Didn't any of you see it?"

"I reached there in time to see Tom Hogan try to stop it and get a ducking for his trouble," laughed Nipper Knapp.

"Oh, it is a shame," continued Bruce; "I know it isn't exactly proper to criticise, but then if they'd had a little system about it old Eli Osborne's barn would still be standing. Now it's a heap of cinders. I tell you any ordinary troop of Boy Scouts has more snap than the Woodbridge Fire Department. I believe— By Jove, fellows. I've an idea! Let's organize a fire department of our own. A motorcycle fire department. I was reading in a magazine only the other day how they started one over in England somewhere. How about it?"

"Bully—how's it done?" demanded Bud Weir, leader of the Blue Heron Patrol.

"Corking idea; let's get busy," exclaimed Jiminy Gordon.

"Great! Give us the details," shouted Romper.

Bruce wrinkled his brow in deep thought for

several moments, then his face lighted up with a smile.

"Look here, fellows," he said enthusiastically, "three of us have motorcycles we got for Christmas, and Romper here and Ray Martin of the Flying Eagles have the machines they built themselves. Then there's 'Old Nanc,' the automobile we built last Winter. She's good enough to carry hose and hatchets and a couple of fellows besides. We've the equipment. What do you say? I'm dead sure my dad will let us borrow some fire extinguishers from the mill, and he has any amount of hose and other things to fit up a first-class brigade. We'll get our equipment together and then drill like the dickens. How about it?"

"And we'll keep it a secret. Won't tell a soul until we get a chance to spring a surprise on the whole town, eh, fellows?" suggested Bud.

"Let's spring it at the tournament and convention next month. The Champlain Valley Firemen's Association meets here this year, you know. Perhaps we can get first prize in the tournament," added Romper Ryan.

"Whoo-o-o-pe! Great! Let's get busy," shouted Nipper Knapp.

"Right-o," said Bruce. "But first of all let's tell our plan to Assistant Scoutmaster Ford."

To be thoroughly familiar with Quarry Troop No. 1 you must know that it was composed of three patrols in Woodbridge, Vt., and that its members had created a reputation for themselves through their ability as mechanics and electricians. Woodbridge has long been noted for its electrically operated marble quarries and its many machine shops and textile mills, and the boys of the town, as a result of their surroundings, were by nature of a mechanical turn. Added to this, the Woodbridge Academy was one of the first institutions of the country to adopt a manual training course as part of its curriculum, and all the lads received an early drilling at the lathes and forges.

Bruce Clifford, always the most self-reliant lad in town, first suggested that he and his fellows establish "a troop of Engineers," and of course his proposal was received with enthusiasm by the

Academy boys.   Bruce took the plan to his father, Samuel Clifford, and to his father's friend, Hamilton Townsend, a well-known consulting engineer in Woodbridge.   Mr. Townsend was delighted with the idea, and quickly consented to become the Scoutmaster, while Mr. Clifford, to foster the interest of the lads along mechanical lines, offered them the abandoned machine shop on the top of Otter Creek Hill for their headquarters.

This was a real find for Bruce and his friends, for the old place had never been dismantled.

Mr. Clifford was a builder of electrical stone cutting and polishing machines and for a long time he had maintained his business in the little two-story structure.   But four years previous he had erected a fine new concrete building just across the way, and abandoned the machine shop, intending to tear down the building and sell the old equipment for junk.

This made ideal headquarters for a troop that desired to specialize in engineering.   On the first floor were the old hand-forges, bellows, lathes, work benches, planing machines, and various other appliances.   They were all out of date, to be sure, and some slightly rusty, but still quite usable after they had been cleaned up.

On the second floor of the building were two rooms, one of which was used for meetings, while the other was converted into a wire room for the loop telegraph line that the lads had built through the town. This loop was connected with an instrument in the bedrooms of every member of the troop and the boys could be routed out of bed at midnight, if need be, by some one calling on any of the keys. A wireless system had also been erected on the roof of the building by the wireless enthusiasts of the troop and the helix, spark-gap and various coils and keys were also set up in the wire room.

Headquarters immediately became popular with every member of the troop and always some one was to be found pottering about in the machine shop, building something that he was particularly interested in. Two of the boys, during the long Winter evenings, had made more or less serviceable motorcycles for themselves, and a half dozen of the young engineers had even essayed the construction of an automobile from old parts they were able to get for "a song" at various junk shops; indeed, some serviceable material was found in scrap heaps about town.

How well they succeeded, a wheezing two-cylinder motor car attested. This turn-out was dubbed "Old Nanc" by the troop, and though it went far better down grade than it did on the level, the boys managed to get a great deal of fun out of it. And it was not a bad looking machine either when it finally received several generous coats of red paint and enamel.

Luckily, Austin Ford, the engineer in charge of the hydro-electric plant of the Woodbridge Quarry Company, became interested in the "Scout Engineers," and through him the officials of the quarry company were persuaded to allow the lads to use as much electric current as they required without cost. The youngsters quickly built a transmission line to the electric station, which was located a few miles north of the town on a branch of Otter Creek.

Mr. Ford's interest in the lads increased to admiration when he saw the business-like way in which they went about building the line, and he even offered them some practical engineering advice when they found themselves up against knotty problems. This led to a more intimate relation with the young Cornell graduate, and in the end the boys suggested that he become the Assistant Scoutmaster. This office rather pleased him, for in reality Austin Ford was little more than a big boy in the matter of pleasure.

He quickly became a master of scout lore and at every opportunity he was afield with the lads or else in the shop at headquarters working out new engineering "stunts" (as he characterized them) for the Scouts to undertake. The boys never failed to talk over each new undertaking with him, as, for instance, the troop's latest scheme, the organization of a motorcycle fire department.

Indeed, on the very evening of the day Eli Osborn's barn was reduced to ashes, Bruce, Bud, Romper and several others visited Mr. Ford and outlined their plans. Of course the Assistant Scoutmaster approved of such a very laudable idea, but he did admonish the boys against criticising the present fire fighting force of Woodbridge, stating that though the men had their pe-culiarities the lads should remember that they were volunteers, doing their work without receiv-ing a cent of pay because they recognized their duty to others.

As to the equipment of the brigade, he left that all up to the boys, telling them, however, that whenever they had any difficulty they would find him ready to help them. He also suggested that they visit the hydro-electric plant and take a few tools and some old sand buckets which they could paint over and use as bucket brigade equipment.

CHAPTER II

THE two weeks following were mighty busy ones for Quarry Troop No. 1. First of all it was necessary for Bruce and his companions to find out exactly what in the matter of equipment they had at their disposal. This could only be determined by a visit to Mr. Clifford's mill and several other places where they could borrow fire fighting apparatus and still not let the news of their secret organization leak out.

Mr. Clifford, when he heard of the plan, was particularly delighted and he personally conducted the boys through the machine shop and mill, making numerous suggestions meanwhile. First of all he found that he could spare eleven small, two-and-one-half gallon chemical extinguishers and still leave enough equipment to comply with the fire underwriters' laws, which call for a certain number of extinguishers for each floor.

These eleven were enough to provide two for

each motorcycle in the brigade and one for the automobile. It seemed rather unfortunate to Bruce that they could only get one for "Old Nanc," for he had had a mental picture of the red automobile with a shining extinguisher on either side of the driver's seat. Indeed, he was so keen on this artistic arrangement that he pleaded with his father to spare an additional tank.

"Why, I'll tell you what you can have to balance up 'Old Nanc,'" said his father laughingly, when he heard Bruce's reason for wanting another extinguisher, "here's a light oxygen-acetylene tank equipment with a blow torch I've been using around the mill. I'm going to get a new one of larger capacity, and if you polish this up it will look mighty business-like, I tell you.

"These torches are being adopted by the city fire departments too. You see they are composed of two tanks, one filled with oxygen and the other with acetylene gas. These gases both flow through the same opening in the torch and unite before they strike the air. If you touch a match to the end of the torch, *presto,* you have a thin blue flame so hot that it will cut through the hardest steel.

The flame gives off a heat as high as 6,000 degrees Fahrenheit; think of that! It literally burns its way through the toughest metal and does the job before you can say 'scat.' The city fire departments use them to burn the hinges off iron doors and window shutters in big warehouse fires. Do you boys want it? It may come in handy, you know.''

''Want it! You bet we do,'' shouted Jiminy Gordon eagerly.

''Just the stuff,'' recommended Romper Ryan, who had been inspecting the apparatus, ''handy and compact. Doesn't weigh more than a hundred pounds. Two of us could handle it in fine shape. We certainly *would* like to have it.''

''All right,'' acquiesced Mr. Clifford, ''it's yours.''

The good-natured manufacturer also gave the boys a set of old fire pails that needed fresh coats of paint, and several lengths of old but serviceable fire hose, not to mention a number of rusty fire hatchets, crowbars and pike poles.

''How about ladders?'' said Mr. Clifford as the boys were about to depart.

"Gee, we never thought of 'em," said Bruce, surprised at such an omission. Then as he considered the capacity of "Old Nanc," he continued: "But if we had them we wouldn't know how to carry them; we—you see, we can't afford to overload the auto or she will never be able to get started for a fire."

"Ho, ho, that's right. She'd be a regular tortoise," said Mr. Clifford. "But why don't you make a couple of scaling ladders? I'll have the top hooks forged for you if you'll build the ladders. They'll be light and serviceable and you can work up a mighty spectacular drill with them."

"Great, we'll do it," said Bruce. Then he added, "perhaps we *will* have a real fire department after all."

"Old Nanc" spent the busiest day of her career gathering up the loads of extinguishers, hose and other equipment before she was laid up for alteration, and the Scouts for many days thereafter found that their spare time was well taken up with their work at headquarters.

From the hour that the Woodbridge Academy closed until ten o'clock in the evening they toiled like beavers. Bruce, always a capable manager, divided the patrols into working squads and assigned them to the various tasks to be accomplished. Those who were handy with carpentering tools he set to work making a new fire patrol body for the automobile. Those who excelled at the forges he assigned to the task of making brackets and metal clamps with which to fasten the extinguishers onto the motorcycles. Some were appointed ladder makers, others were painters, and still others were buffers and polishers, who shined up the tarnished sides of the tanks and took the rust off the axes and pike heads. And when they all became active the interior of headquarters was a veritable beehive for busyness.

The boys did not devote all their time to building work, however, for they realized that to win honors at the firemen's tournament, in which they meant to compete, they would have to be well drilled in every branch of fire fighting. Consequently every evening, just before dusk, the entire troop assembled in the field back of headquarters.

Scaling ladder drills, first aid work, rescue

work, bucket brigade drills, and hose coupling con
tests were indulged in until the lads worked with
the precision and accuracy of trained fire fighters.
For the sake of unity Bruce had been appointed
fire chief, having charge of all three patrols. The
entire squad was under his command and in a very
few days he had systematized their work to the
point where there was scarcely a lost motion or a
false move.

Indeed, the Scouts drilled with such vigor and
enthusiasm that inside of an hour they would be
completely tired out. Then, while they were resting, Bruce would put them through a sharp oral
drill on the rudiments of firemanship as set forth
in the September number of *Boy's Life* until, to
quote Jiminy Gordon, ''They could say it back-
wards, or upside down, and do it blindfolded.''

Gradually after weeks of toil the fleet of fire
fighting motorcycles assumed a business-like appearance. And as for ''Old Nanc'' she, redolent
with the odors of fresh red paint, loomed above
them all exactly like a mother hen keeping a watch-
ful eye on her brood of chicks.

Each motorcycle was equipped with a fire extinguisher clamped on either side, just back of the seat. Directly in the rear of the seat was a small red tool box in which hose-coupling wrenches and two sets of harness were kept. This harness, devised by Mr. Ford, was made of canvas in the form of a sling to hold the extinguishers in position on a Scout's back. In that way a boy could enter a burning building and carry an extinguisher with him, still having both hands free to operate the extinguisher hose. On top of the tool box was strapped a short coil of hose with a small nozzle ready to be brought into action when coupled to the nearest street hydrant.

"Old Nanc," besides carrying an extinguisher and the oxygen-acetylene blow torch tank, also contained the remaining hose, an equipment of axes, pike poles and scaling ladders, and provided accommodations for three Scouts and the driver besides.

Until a few days before the tournament the Scouts were working on their equipment. Indeed, the very last coat of varnish was put onto "Old Nanc" the Saturday afternoon preceding the tournament day, which fell on Wednesday. All

that remained to be done was to deck the machine
with flags and bunting and she would be ready
for the parade.   In truth, that very morning Bruce
had gone on a motorcycle trip to St. Cloud City,
twelve miles south of Woodbridge, to buy the necessary decorations.

"By Jove, she looks like a real fire fighter,
doesn't she?" said Romper Ryan, backing off,
paint brush still in hand, to survey his own handi-
work on the sides of "Old Nanc."

"For downright good looks I think our equipment has it on anything Woodbridge ever
experienced," said Jiminy Gordon enthusiastically.

"Well, we'll sure create some sensation," said
Bud. "This is going to be a complete surprise to
everybody. Has Bruce heard from Chief Blaney
yet? He sent him our entry for the tournament
events last week, you know. I wonder— Here
he comes now! I heard his siren. That was a
mighty quick trip to St. Cloud."

Bud and several others rushed to the door.
Coming up the hill at top speed was Bruce, his
motorcycle fairly flying. When he caught sight

of the group in front of the machine shop he began to wave a blue paper above his head.

"Hi, fellows, here's our reply from Chief Blaney," he shouted as he jumped from his machine. "I just got it at the house. Haven't opened it yet. Come on, gather 'round and hear what he has to say."

With eager fingers he tore off the corner of the big envelope and ripped open the top. And as he unfolded the letter every Scout pressed closer to get a glimpse of its contents. Bruce began to read aloud:

Mr. Bruce Clifford, Chief of the Scout Engineers' Fire Department.

DEAR SIR: Your entry blank and fee for the tournament events reached me. I am returning your fee herewith for, unfortunately, your company cannot take part in the tournament. In the first place your organization is only a juvenile company, and in the second place it is not an accredited member of the Woodbridge Fire Department.

The fact that you have not a charter from the town authorities will also prevent your little department from taking an active part in fighting fires in this village, for the Champlain Valley Volunteer Firemen's Association has passed a ruling preventing any individual not wearing a badge of a recognized fire department from entering fire lines or participating in fire fighting work. These rules are rigidly enforced by my department.   Very truly yours,

(Signed) W. T. BLANEY,
Chief Woodbridge F. D.

"Well, what do you think of that!" exclaimed Romper disgustedly.

"And after all our working and planning," said Jiminy bitterly.

"Oh, we're only juveniles," said Bud sarcastically, turning away to hide his feelings.

And as for Bruce, he could hardly believe his eyes. He re-read the letter and when he finished he slowly tore it into little scraps and tossed them to the ground.

"Well, fellows," he said with a grim smile, "I fancy 'Old Nanc' won't need the flags and bunting I ordered to-day. And I guess our little fire department sort of busts up before it gets started. If old Blaney is such a stickler for regulations they'll never let us fight any fires in this town. Tough luck, isn't it?"

Tournament day had been declared a holiday in Woodbridge. Stores and factories were closed and the village decorated from stable to Town Hall with colored streamers, flags and bunting. Since early morning fire companies had been arriving in town headed by bands and drum corps until the place was crowded with uniformed figures from every section of Vermont.

But in spite of all this gaiety Bruce Clifford and the Boy Scout Engineers were dispirited. Indeed, for the past week they had been very unhappy over the turn of affairs. They tried their hardest to brace up and be good sports, but their disappointment was greater than they had expected. On tournament day they wandered about with a cheerless air, watching the various companies file into the side streets to await the formation of the parade that would be conducted up Webster Avenue to the tournament grounds.

They were not so downcast, however, as to ignore the fact that here was an excellent opportunity to view a number of fire fighting machines of all varieties. Indeed, they inspected the equipment of every out-of-town company they ran across, and in the course of the morning had become partly familiar with everything, from an old-fashioned gooseneck hand engine to the latest type of hand-drawn chemical engine, the pride of the company from Middlebury. This last appliance was an excellent piece of work and Bruce and his friends realized that even with her new paint and shining brass, "Old Nanc" could not compare in general appearance with this costly equipment.

Promptly at half-past ten the automobile in which was seated the Mayor, Fire Chief Blaney and several other dignitaries, swung into Webster avenue. This was followed by the Woodbridge band and the parade to the tournament grounds was under way. The Boy Scout Engineers reviewed the procession from the curb, and when it had passed they hurried by way of a short cut across the fields to the tournament grounds, reaching there just as the Mayor's car turned in at the big gate.

A makeshift two-story frame building had been constructed in the very center of the enclosure, and the village authorities had erected a dozen temporary hydrants in a half circle about the front of the building. The plan was to conduct the contests on the level stretch of turf before the grandstand, and as a finale set fire to the wooden structure and have a real demonstration of fire fighting.

The procession of visiting companies made a

circle of the grounds after entering the gate while the Mayor reviewed them from his automobile. Then after the various engines and hose carts had been parked at the far end of the field the Mayor prepared formally to open the ceremonies with a speech of welcome. But he had hardly uttered two sentences when Bruce, for some unknown reason turned and looked down Webster avenue towards the town. In the distance he saw a great cloud of black smoke mounting skyward above the roofs. He grasped Bud Weir's arm and shouted:

"Look! Quick! A fire!"

And as if to verify his words the far-off clang of the village fire bell sounded.

Instantly the tournament grounds were in a turmoil. Every one raised a cry of fire! In a twinkle the grandstand was empty, but before the crowd could reach Webster avenue the companies had begun to leave the enclosure. With a rattle and a clang one engine after another swung into the broad avenue. Then with the old hand equipment of the Woodbridge vamps in the van the whole aggregation hurled itself down the street toward the village.

CHAPTER III

BRUCE CLIFFORD and the other members of Quarry Troop No. 1, waited only to determine the location of the column of smoke that now extended clear across the sky, then, selecting the short cut across the field by which they had come, they hurried pellmell toward the scene of trouble.

"It's down in the factories!" panted Romper as he ran.

"Yes, I think it's Mayor Worthington's woolen mills," shouted Bud.

"By Jove, I guess you're right," yelled Bruce, as they turned into Willow Street and saw smoke pouring from the windows of the big brick building at the far end of the street.

It was the worst fire that Woodbridge had experienced in years. By the time the firemen reached the scene the whole west end of the building was enveloped in flames and a section of the slate roof had already caved in.   From every window long tongues of red flames darted out like hideous serpents' tongues. Great sparks shot skyward as sections of the west wall crumbled and fell into the red hot caldron that had once been the building's interior, and the heat was so intense that windows in the factory building across the street cracked and crumbled.

It was a fortunate thing for Woodbridge that there was a score of visiting fire companies in town, or else the whole south section of the village would have been wiped out.   Chief Blaney, almost beside himself with anxiety, implored the visiting chiefs for their assistance.   And assist him they did.   Every company got its equipment into action and lines of hose were strung in some cases nearly half a mile.   There were at least a dozen hand engines and two steamers on the banks of Otter Creek supplying lines to the fire, not to mention the hundreds of feet of hose that were coupled to the village hydrant system in every direction.

But all that the willing vamps could do seemed to no avail.   The fire demon was rampant.   He roared full cry through the long brick building, consuming everything in his path. Section after section of roof sagged, then fell with a crash and a roar into the flames, sending aloft a shower of crackling sparks.

"Thank heavens, this was a holiday. There's no one in the building," Bruce heard Chief Blaney cry as he hurried past in company with the foreman of a visiting company.

But the rubber-coated fire fighter had hardly uttered the words when a shout went up from the crowd at the east end of the building, where the firm's office was located.   Men with blanched faces and trembling hands were pointing towards the big iron barred window that marked the counting room.

"O-o-h! It's old Uriah Watkins!" shrieked Blaney.

Bruce looked and turned sick at the sight. There, his wrinkled old face pressing against the bars, was the aged bookkeeper of the woolen mills. One hand was extended between the iron grating in frantic appeal.   The other clutched the precious ledgers that the old man had rashly rushed into the building to rescue. His ashen face was set with a horrible expression, and his eyes stood out with terror. Bruce saw his lips move, but could not hear his feeble voice above the roar of the flames.

For a moment the scout stood panic stricken. Then suddenly his lips pressed together and his face took on a determined look. In a flash he turned to Bud and gave a few brief orders. Then, elbowing their way through the jam and press about them, the youngsters disappeared and left Bruce there alone.

In the meantime a score of vamps had been summoned by Chief Blaney to rescue the aged bookkeeper. They attacked the heavy bars on the window with sledges and axes, but with no success. They tried to pry away the bricks with crowbars, but this, too, failed, and it was quite apparent to all that if Uriah Watkins was to be saved it could be accomplished only by the slow and laborious task of sawing through the bars. Could this be done? Had they the time to accomplish the task?

Already a nearby section of the roof had caved in! How long would it be before the flames reached the office and burned the old man alive?

At this point the figure of a boy in Scout uniform broke through the fire lines and rushed up to the side of Chief Blaney. Standing at attention, Bruce saluted in regulation Boy Scout fashion and asked briefly:

"Chief, can the Boy Scout Engineers take a hand in this? I'll have the bars cut in two minutes."

"You will what—! Why—!"

"Yes, yes, we can do it; I've sent for our fire department—here come the Scouts now!"

The shriek of sirens was heard above the din about the factory building and the great crowd beheld seven motorcycles tearing down the hill at top speed. And just behind them bowled "Old Nanc" at her best.

"Have I your permission to take a hand?" demanded Bruce.

"Yes! yes! for goodness' sake do anything you can to free him!" cried the chief.

The line of motorcycles stopped and hose lines

were quickly strung. But the red automobile
rumbled on, to come to a halt within ten yards of
the building. Already two scouts were unlimber-
ing the oxyhydrogen tanks and blow pipe equipment. Bruce rushed forward to aid them, while
Chief Blaney looked on quite puzzled for the moment.

Working fast, but with the utmost coolness,
Bruce donned a pair of asbestos gloves that came
with the equipment and attached the blow pipe.
Romper turned on the gases, while the young
leader produced a match and ignited the torch.
Instantly a tiny blue flame shot out that hissed
and sputtered in a threatening manner.

As he advanced toward the window Bruce saw
that the old bookkeeper had disappeared. He
knew from this that there was no time to be lost,
for the man had probably fainted and would soon
be overcome with smoke. Hastily he shot the
blue flame at the base of the first bar. There was
a hiss and a shower of sparks as the flame met the
cold metal. Bruce pressed the blow pipe closer,
while he watched with anxious eye the progress
of the flame.

The bar grew red, then gold, then white. The heat was terrific. The bar began to melt, slowly first, then faster, until the blue flame ate completely through. Another was attacked, and still another, until the scout had cut a hole in the iron grating large enough for a man to pass through.

Shouting to Romper to turn off the gas, he dropped the blow pipe, and plunging a handkerchief in a fire pail that stood near by, he tied the cloth over his nose and mouth. Then he hoisted himself through the window and disappeared.

Inside the smoke was thick and black, but Bruce could see flames dart through at the far end of the room, and he knew that in a few moments more the place would be seething.

He groped vainly about for the old bookkeeper. Where was he? He had dropped under the window a moment ago. Had he tried to crawl to the door? What had happened?

The smoke was so thick that even the moist handkerchief was of no avail. Bruce began to strangle. Then suddenly he remembered the instructions in his Handbook. The air was purest near the floor!

He dropped to his hands and knees, and with his face to the boards he began to crawl about, blindly groping for the body of the old bookkeeper. His fingers clutched something. He drew the object toward him and peered at it through the smoke. It was Uriah Watkins doubled in a ball, and though unconscious and almost suffocated, the faithful old man still clasped his precious ledgers.

Bruce knew that unless the man reached the open air immediately he would perish. Also he knew that if they were not both clear of the building in a few minutes they would be food for the flames which were even then thrusting spiteful tongues under the door at the other end of the room.

Here again the instructions of the Handbook stood the scout in good stead. He knew that it would be next to suicide to stand up and try to carry the prostrated form to the window. The smoke was so thick even down there near the floor that he was gasping and choking.

He twisted his hand into the old man's collar and began to crawl, face to the floor, back toward the gray space that marked the window through the smoke, hauling Uriah after him. Foot by foot he dragged his burden. In spite of the handkerchief the smoke was getting into his lungs. His chest pained him dreadfully. Oh, what wouldn't he give for a single breath of pure, fresh air! The eight or ten feet to the side wall seemed like eight or ten miles. Would he never reach there!

Finally his hand struck the wall and he stood erect. The draught caused by the open window was drawing thick smoke out of the building into the air. Bruce knew he could not stand in that current of gases long. Pulling Uriah Watkins forward, he raised the limp form and forced it through the window ahead of him. Willing hands seized the old bookkeeper and lifted him to safety.

Then, dizzy and sick, Bruce clutched at the ledge and scrambled up. But a dreadful nausea seized him as he knelt on the window sill. His head whirled. He lost his balance. He knew he was falling backward into the burning building, but he was powerless to save himself. He gave a stifled cry of terror, and in answer the loud voice of Chief

He raised the limp form and forced it through the
window.   (Page 40) *Frontispiece*

Blaney boomed in his ear and strong arms encircled his waist. Then everything grew black.

The Boy Scout Engineers never forgot the shout that went up when Chief Blaney carried the unconscious form of Bruce to safety. They were mighty proud of their leader. But they were prouder still when, a week later, Bruce was summoned into the presence of Mayor Worthington and Chief Blaney and presented with a parchment charter which officially informed him that the fire company of Quarry Troop had been officially made a member of the Woodbridge Fire Department, to be known thereafter as Chemical Company No. 1, with Brewster W. Clifford as the Chief.

CHAPTER IV

WHEN THE CIRCUS CAME TO TOWN

TWELVE Scouts, nearly half of Quarry Troop No. 1, now popularly known as the Boy Scout Engineers, were gathered in the meeting room at headquarters. In fact, they had been literally driven there when the Woodbridge Academy let out at half past two on Friday afternoon. You see, it was raining so hard that there was no other place to go. But, then, the old machine shop was the best place in the world for the boys, rain or shine, so *that* didn't make much difference. What really did matter was the monotony of it all. For five days now the region round about Woodbridge had been literally deluged with a spring downpour. Otter Creek had swollen to twice its normal size, springs were gushing from most unheard-of places and rivulets were racing down hillsides that usually were, to quote Nipper Knapp, "dry as a smoked herring."

"By George, I do wish this rain would let up. What we want is a chance to get out of doors a bit. I haven't stretched my legs in a week," said Romper Ryan glumly, as he gazed out of the big front window.

"Well," said fat Babe Wilson with his usual sarcasm, "if it don't dry up soon the whole blamed world is liable to shrink." Then, as an after thought, he added, "That might bring St. Cloud City so near Woodbridge that we could at least see the circus parade."

"Aw-w, what'er you bringing up that circus subject for again," said Jiminy Gordon, who didn't like to be reminded of the pleasure he had decided to forego.

"Yes," chorused two others who were equally reluctant about facing the sacrifice they had voted themselves; "forget about that blooming circus."

"Say, you fellows needn't hop on me just because I want to have a little fun with you," protested Babe. "I'm as good a sport as any of you. Don't you suppose I agreed when you voted not to go to the circus. I know it would be foolish to spend most of the thirty dollars in the troop's treasury for a day's outing. You needn't talk, Jiminy Gordon; you were the first one to suggest the idea last week when you saw the man posting the bills.''

"Yes, I know I was," said Jiminy, somewhat embarrassed, "but I said it without thinking. When we got to discussing it last night I saw how ridiculous it was. By Jiminy, I'd rather see the money go toward a new camping outfit, or the lumber for the troop's power boat. I wouldn't spend that thirty dollars to see three circuses, I wouldn't.''

Judging from the conversation, the circus question referred to had died a hard death. To tell the truth, its demise had really been quite painful so far as most of the boys were concerned, for all of them had rather liked the idea of being able to enjoy "the World's Mightiest, Most Magnificent Combination of Clever Animals and Human Skill and Daring," etc., which was booked to show in St. Cloud City a few days hence.

For a week the temptation to spend the troop's thirty dollars had haunted the lads day and night, until finally with a great effort they had laid the ghost by a unanimous vote that the money must not be spent on the profitless amusement. It really was a sacrifice, for every Scout had set his heart on a hike to St. Cloud and a day crowded full of gaiety and glitter, not to mention a stomach crowded fuller with peanuts, popcorn and lemonade.

"Fellows, I am just as much disappointed as the rest," said Bruce Clifford, leader of the Owl patrol, "but I think we decided wisely last night. We can all do without going to the circus, even if it is the biggest one that has visited this neck of the woods in years. The possibility of a new set of tents or the lumber for a motorboat appeals to me more than blowing the money in on a show; that is, it does when I stop and think soberly about it."

"Right-o!" said Romper.

"That's what I call common sense," asserted Nipper Knapp.

"Just the way we all should look at it," insisted Bud Weir, leader of the Blue Heron patrol.

"And if we were to—sh! Listen, fellows!

Some one's calling!'' In an instant everybody was silent.

Bruce inclined his head toward the wire room at the other end of the building where the headquarters' telegraph key and the instruments connected with the wireless aerials on the roof were located.   Out of the doorway seemed to tumble a confusion of dots and dashes quite unintelligible to any one not familiar with the Morse International Code.

.... — . — , ... — . — , .. — . — .. — . — ..
— .. — —.

''Heaquarters, Ford calling,'' read Bruce. ''Fellows, Mr. Ford is trying to raise us.   Wonder what he wants!''

He hurried into the wire room with the rest at his heels, and taking the low operator's chair opened the key and answered the call.   Then he closed it again and waited.   The boys were all attention, for most of them were second-class scouts and could ''read'' Morse well.

''Mayor — Worthington — just — 'phoned — me,'' clicked the instrument.   ''Wants — to — see — Scouts — at — Town — Hall — at — four — 1

— would — like — to — have — you — go.— Ford
— Asst — S'ct — M's't'r — 3:10 — p — m.''

''All — right — Shall — we — wear — uniforms
— Bruce — L'd'r — Owl — P't'r'l — 3:12 — p —
m,'' Bruce flashed back over the wire.

''Yes — careful — don't — get — too — wet —
G'd — by — Ford — 3:14 — p — m,'' came the
answer.

''Cracky! Something interesting! Wonder
what's up!'' said Bruce excitedly, as he began
calling on the loop telegraph wire that was connected to an instrument in every Scout's home.

The three patrols of Quarry Troop stood at attention in the broad corridor of the Woodbridge
Town Hall, awaiting the coming of Mayor Worthington. Their campaign hats were water-soaked,
and rain dripped from the edge of their slickers
and gathered in little pools about their feet. They
must have been uncomfortable. But if they were,
they gave no signs of it. All their attention was
riveted on the doors that led the way into the
Mayor's private office.

Presently these doors swung open, and the tall,
broad-shouldered figure of the town's chief ex-

ecutive strode forth, followed by his secretary and
Timothy Cockran, the Commissioner of Streets
and Highways. Every back stiffened and every
hand went up in salute as these men advanced and
took their position in front of Bruce, the recognized spokesman of the troop. The Mayor ac-
knowledged the salute in quite the proper manner,
as did the others; then, clearing his throat, he
spoke.

"Scouts, I have asked you here because you can
be of service to Woodbridge. The town needs
you. Are you willing to do a good turn for the
welfare of us all?"

"We're ready for anything, sir. We try to do
a good turn daily, rain or shine," said Bruce, once
more saluting.

And his answer was echoed by the score or more
of brown-clad youths ranged in line beside him.

"Thank you, Scouts," said Mr. Worthington,
crisply. "Now to business. The rains of the last
few days have raised havoc in this end of Champlain Valley. So much water has fallen that the
high roads leading north and south on either side
of the valley have been made dangerous by wash-

outs and landslides. In several places the banks
have slipped down from above, but the most dangerous sections are those where the roads have
been washed away almost entirely. Vehicles traveling at night are very apt to have serious upsets
and the life and limb of the occupants are endan-
gered, in spite of the fact that we have marked
the washouts with red lanterns hung on short
posts.

"What I would like to have you boys do is to
organize a road patrol to keep a careful watch
over these red lamps and see that they are all
lighted between the hours of nightfall and midnight at least. After twelve o'clock there is
hardly enough traffic to make the patrolling worth
while. The first patrol can light the lamps at a
given hour and thereafter at certain intervals
Scout patrols can visit each lamp and see that it
is in good working order. How would you like
the job, boys?"

"Fine!" shouted some.

"Just the kind of work we like," cried others.

"All right," said the Mayor, shortly. "Scouts,
you are hereby appointed Guardians of the High-

ways by order of the Mayor and the Commissioner of Streets and Highways. Each morning at half past eight one of your number will be expected to make a report at the Town Hall of the night's work.

"The Commissioner here has a map of these thoroughfares showing each washout and just where each lamp is located. You can organize your patrols this afternoon and start to-night. I think the storm will be somewhat abated by that time. It is letting up a little now. Good-day and good luck."

Though the rain had decreased considerably the Scouts lost little time in getting from the Town Hall to Scout headquarters, where the details of organizing the road patrols were worked out. It required the rest of the afternoon to do this, and the dinner hour arrived almost before the boys were aware of the time.

"Say, fellows, this is going to be fine," said Bud Weir. Then, glancing out of the window, he exclaimed: "By Jove, the storm's nearly over; the clouds are breaking out there beyond the mountains. This will be a fine night for—

Cracky, fellows, I almost forgot; the circus comes through town to-night. It will come down the valley from Collinsville and take the north road to St. Cloud.''

"By George, you're right," exclaimed Bruce. "Say, fellows, that makes our work doubly important. These heavy circus vans may get into trouble if all the lamps aren't in good order. You fellows be sure and report for duty, will you?"

"Don't worry; there'll be enough of us to patrol to-night. I guess we're all going to stay up and see the circus go through town, if it isn't raining, aren't we, fellows?" asked Bud. And from the chorus of affirmatives it was evident that few of the troop would be abed when the "World's Mightiest, Most Magnificent Combination of Clever Animals and Human Skill and Daring" rumbled through town.

By seven o'clock the rain had stopped entirely and, when the lamp-lighting patrols started out in the gloaming, the storm clouds were fast disappearing in the southwest, their edges splashed with the gold and vermilion fire of the setting sun.

Indeed, by the time the second patrol had re-

ported back at headquarters and the third group
of night watchers had started out, a big yellow
moon had appeared and the stars were twinkling
merrily up above.

After the last patrol had been gone an hour the
Scouts who, when their duties were finished, had
gathered in headquarters, moved on to the top of
Otter Creek hill. They had decided that this
would be the best place to watch the coming of the
circus cavalcade.

The valley presented a queer appearance at
that hour.   Here and there were red lights standing out against the darkness, while from various
points along the highway came the glow of tiny
battery lamps as the Scouts signaled to each other.

"They look like a lot of fireflies," said Bruce,
after he had watched the series of dots and dashes
that the boys were flashing back and forth.

"Yes," said Bud, "just like mighty big fli—.
Hi, fellows, here comes the circus! See 'em—
that string of lights coming down Willow Street—
hear that rumble of the wagons?"

"Sure enough!" exclaimed Bruce, who was as
enthusiastic as the rest.

Up the long hill, in view of the group of wide-eyed and thoroughly interested boys, came the phantom-like caravan. A string of swinging lanterns fastened to the center pole of each wagon marked its course.

First in line were the grumbling and rumbling red and blue animal vans, followed by two rattling canvas wagons. Then a troop of little black and white ponies appeared hitched in fours to light gilt and red vehicles that held all sorts of odds and ends. In the rear of the ponies followed the camels; great, long-legged creatures that grunted at every stride as if they were indignant at being kept up so late. Gaudy band wagons, the cook's outfit and a heterogeneous assortment of vehicles came next, all of them moving slowly up the hill while the drivers dozed in their seats.

"Say, isn't it great?" cried Romper Ryan as he took in every little detail.

"You bet it is!" returned Babe Wilson, breathlessly. "I wonder where the elephants are. Oh, here they come!"

The clank of chains could be heard above the grumble of the wagons, and a moment later five huge elephants appeared out of the darkness. They lumbered along sleepily, their massive heads and long trunks swaying from side to side at every stride. The forelegs of each beast were chained together with stout links of iron, but there was little need of fetters, for the animals were apparently so docile that the idea of running away seemed farthest from their minds. The leader of the drove was, of course, the largest and apparently the meekest, for as he scuffled by the Scouts the boys saw that he walked with his tiny eyes closed exactly as if he were asleep.

A string of a dozen red vans followed the elephants, and at the very rear of the line was the big steam calliope. It was muffled and silent now, out its driver was snoring lustily as if to keep its reputation.

"Gee, but that was worth staying up to see," said Ray Martin, the first to find his tongue, after the cavalcade had passed on down the valley.

"You bet it was," said Bruce. "Jove, I'm almost sorry we decided— Say! Look! Something has happened! See the lights down there by the old quarry hole? The circus has stopped!

Look, there are some signals! It's the patrol! Can you read them?"

" 'We — need — help. — Elephant — in — in—' What the dickens is he talking about? I couldn't get that last, could you, Bruce?" asked Bud Weir.

"Yes; he said that an elephant is in the quarry hole. By George, one of those big beasts has fallen down into Tollen's old quarry. There was ⁻ washout down there. Come on, fellows!"

And the Scouts started at top speed down the North Valley road toward the scene of trouble.

CHAPTER V

BEDLAM reigned at the quarry hole. A score of frantic circus men were shouting orders at each other, lanterns were bobbing about among the wagons, and every one was beside himself with excitement. One little gray-haired man seemed almost distraught over the situation. He was storming up and down the road, alternately roaring commands and delivering tirades against everything in general. It was quite evident that he was the manager of the outfit.

"Now we're in a fine mess," he thundered as he strode to the edge of the quarry and peered down into the darkness. "It's so dogon dark down there we can't even see th' brute. How'll we ever get him out? That's what I want to know. Hang the man who's responsible for this mess! Gol-ding t'—*wush—phew.*"

His soliloquy on the brink of the quarry hole ended abruptly when with a snort the elephant shot a trunk full of water out of the darkness, bowling the little man over and drenching everything and everybody.

"Kill t' beast! Kill him, Gol—ding his hide!" screamed the dripping manager as he picked himself up out of the mud. But he was such a comical figure that every one shouted with laughter.

To Bruce and the Scouts the whole situation was extremely humorous. Evidently the lead elephant had wandered into the washout and lost his footing. The next thing he knew he had slid with a big splash into the quarry hole. And then, having a fondness for water and seeing no way to climb up the twenty-foot wall of rocks, he had decided to stay there and have a thoroughly good time.

But Bruce realized that they could not indulge their humor long, for as guardians of the road it was their duty to give all the assistance they could. Hastily the patrol leader made an inspection of the pit by the light of his pocket flash. He remembered a derrick on one side of the cut, and he hastened to look that over, for already he was beginning to form plans for getting the beast out of trouble.

He noted with satisfaction that the derrick had been only partly dismantled and that the rusty steel cable was coiled up in a pile beside the heavy upright. Then he returned to the roadside and approached the agitated little manager.

"We are the Guardians of the Highways for Woodbridge, sir," he said, "and we would—"

"You are the WHAT!" roared the manager.

"The Guardians of the Highways and—"

"Well, why in tarnation didn't yuh guard 'em then? I—I—I—"

Bruce interrupted the sputtering manager by pointing to the red light.

"There's our light. We did our part. It must have been your fault. But no matter; we'll help you get the animal out of the quarry if you'll let us."

"How'll yuh do it? Haven't got a thing in my outfit t' pull him out with."

"Oh, we'll do it all right," said Bruce. Then briefly he outlined his plan to the skeptical circus manager. And when he had finished talking the old man looked at him in amazement.

"Can you do all that?" he demanded.

"Sure we can," said Bruce. "We're the Boy Scout Engineers. Just loan me some of your canvas men who know how to rig a block and tackle and we'll have the elephant on his way to St. Cloud by daylight at the latest."

"All right, I'll go you," said the manager.

Bruce gathered about him all the Scouts not doing patrol duty.

"Fellows," he said, "we can get the elephant out of the hole all right, but it will mean some hard work. I want you, Romper, to go back to Woodbridge and tell the parents of every fellow here that we have serious work to do. Tell them not to worry if we don't get back until late. Then I want the Owl Patrol to go to headquarters and get all the No. 10 wire we have on hand, load it on a couple of wheelbarrows and start stringing a line from our switchboard in the machine shop down to the quarry hole here.

"String it along the fences and where you have to cross Druery road put it overhead from tree

to tree. Remember, no monkeying with the telegraph or telephone poles! We can be arrested
for anything like that. Romper, you can stop
in and ask Mr. Ford if he won't go up to Headquarters and connect up the new line. I don't
think we should fuss with the switchboard at
night.

"Now, I want the Blue Herons to go to headquarters and disconnect the big five-horsepower
motor on the lathe. Load it aboard 'Old Nanc'
and bring it down here as fast as you can. On
your way turn in at Druery road and run up to
the Baldwin quarries. Ask Dave Porter, the night
foreman there, if you can borrow the largest and
heaviest blasting mat he has. We'll need that.
Now hurry, fellows."

The Scouts started off immediately, and Bruce
turned to the circus manager.

"Now, if you'll bring your canvas men along,
I'll give them a good, hard job. It's one we boys
couldn't handle. Are you ready?"

"Sure!" said the manager. Then to his men,
"Come on, boys!"

Bruce led the group around the quarry hole to

the north side and pointed out the derrick and the coil of rusted steel cable.

"Here's what we'll lift the elephant out with, providing the boom will hold and your men can string the heavy cable through the pulleys at night."

"Huh! our end of it is no trick for a bunch of canvasbacks," said the foreman of the gang. "Get busy, boys; quick now! Some of you bring some gasoline torches so's we kin see! Move now, you fellers!"

In five minutes the circus men were working like beavers, weaving the cable through the pulleys, placing the heavy boom and getting the derrick fitted up for service. The system and speed with which the trained tent riggers went about their task was nothing short of marvelous to Bruce. He watched them almost fascinated until the little manager came up and claimed his attention.

"Look here you feller, I ain't sure your scheme is goin' t' work out," said he, skeptically. "How'er we goin' t' get some light into t' hole t' see the brute? These gasoline torches can't be

lowered down there.   The elephant would go wild
and probably drowned hisself, an' if—"

"I'm figuring on using the headlights of Old
Nanc (that's the troop's automobile we built last
winter) for searchlights.   They are powerful
enough and can be turned anywhere we need 'em.
There, you can get a look at them now.   That's
Old Nanc on her way here."

Up the road sounded a siren, and the little manager turned to see two headlights bowling toward
him.   It was Old Nanc loaded down with the
heavy motor, blasting mat and tools.

"Fine, Bud; you made a fast trip.   How
are the wire stringers getting along?" shouted
Bruce to the Scout who was driving the machine.

"We passed them about a hundred and fifty
yards from here.   They are coming along in fine
shape."

"Good," said Bruce.   "Now bring Old Nanc
right up to the edge of the quarry hole.   We want
to shine her headlights down into there and see
what it looks like below.   Some of the circus men
can unload the motor, and Nipper, you can show

them how to set it up on the derrick platform. And while all this is going on, Babe, you take charge of making a sling. Take this blasting mat and get a couple of circus men to help you bend a section of cable to each of the four corners. Fasten the ends together around that rusty derrick hook attached to the end of the cable. Hurry it, will you, fellows?"

With the help of some of the "canvas-backs," the automobile was worked off of the road and into the field on the north side of the quarry hole near the derrick. Then it was pushed cautiously toward the edge of the pit and its wheels blocked by some big pieces of marble so that it would not roll into the hole. The rays of the headlights dispelled the darkness below immediately and there was His Highness the Elephant, almost submerged, looking up at them with his ridiculously small eyes.

"Huh! Consarn it! I *knew* you kids was playin' me fer a fool," roared the circus manager when he looked into the cut. "How'er you're goin' to hitch anything around *that* animal, I'd like to know?"

"We don't intend to hitch anything around him. We're going to make a sling of that big blasting mat and raise him out that way."

"Yes!" roared the furious manager, "but how in tarnation are you going to get it *under* his belly? Think some one is going down there and dive between his legs with your blooming old sling, do yuh? That animal is nearly all under water, remember."

To tell the truth, that question *had* been bothering Bruce from the first. He had hoped that the water was only two or three feet deep. But there was at least ten feet of drainage in the quarry hole! He stood beside Old Nanc and bit his lips in his embarrassment. Luck seemed against him. Was everything going to fall through at the last moment?

He did not answer the irate manager, but began to turn one of the headlights slowly so its rays illuminated the west wall of the hole. Then suddenly the light paused, and a smile crept over the boy's face. The white beams had revealed to him a shelf of marble two feet above the water-line and at least ten feet across, skirting the lower edge of the west wall.   He saw defeat turned into victory!

"Will that elephant mind his trainer?" Bruce demanded of the manager.

"Huh! Will he? Well, you'd better guess he will!" stormed the man.

"Then everything is simple. You lower the trainer in a bo'son's chair over the west wall there and down to that ledge of marble. He can coax the animal out of the water and up on the rocks, and after that we can send a couple more men down with the sling and they can do the rest. See the plan?"

"Well, I'll be hanged! You win, young feller," said the manager, smiling for the first time since the accident.

At this point the lads of the Owl Patrol reached the quarry hole trundling several empty wheel-barrows. Jiminy Gordon was carrying the remains of the last roll of wire.

"Here we are, Bruce, ready to connect up, but you'd better believe building a line at night is no easy job, by Jiminy."

"Guess it isn't," said Bruce in a businesslike tone. "Is Mr. Ford at headquarters?"

"Yes, he's waiting to turn on the current whenever he gets your signal."

"Great!" said Bruce. "I was a little worried about that. There isn't any real danger, but you might have made a ground or a short circuit and upset everything." Then turning to Nipper Knapp, he shouted, "How about the motor, Nipper?"

"Set and ready for connections," shouted the Scout.

"Right-o! Then we'll have Mr. Elephant out of the hole in a jiffy," shouted Bruce, as he seized the two ends of the wires and began to bend them about the terminals of the motor. He worked with speed and accuracy and the little circus manager could not help commenting on his skill as an electrician.

"Hum! I guess you lads know what you're doin', all right," he said.

"Well, we hope our efforts are successful," said Bruce. Then he added, "It's time you sent your trainer down there on the ledge to get the elephant out of the water."

"Don't worry, son; we ain't losin' no time on

our end of this game. He's down there now an'—"

Shouts of laughter from the crowd assembled around the edge of the hole interrupted the little manager.

He and Bruce both looked up involuntarily. Then they, too, burst into uproarious laughter at the spectacle.

The trainer had gone down onto the ledge with an armful of bread loaves to tempt the elephant out of the water. There he stood holding out a loaf invitingly while the elephant, still half submerged, held his great mouth open and his trunk aloft expecting the man to toss the bread toward him. But this was not the trainer's intention.

"Come on, Toby; come on. Yuh gotta come out t' git this meal," he called.

The elephant moved a little closer and waved his trunk aloft impatiently as if beckoning the trainer to toss the loaf.

"Oh, no, yuh don't. Come on out, Toby; come on— Hi! Gol ding yuh, leggo!— Hi! *Help!* Help!"

Toby had refused to be tempted any longer.

The waving trunk descended and wrapped quickly about the trainer's leg. Then slowly the animal began to pull the man toward the water. The trainer was startled half to death. He dropped the bread and began to struggle mightily, for the black water looked cold to him even though the elephant did seem to enjoy it. He clutched at the smooth marble floor and tried to brace himself with his unincumbered leg, shouting lustily all the time.

"Hi! help me! Help! Kill th' beast! I don' wanna git a duckin'! I—I—got a cold in—my—"
Splash—blub—blub—blub—

Toby's black little eyes seemed to twinkle with mischief as he gave a final tug and plunged the trainer into the water. Then while the man floundered about, the animal deliberately put his two front feet onto the edge of the shelf and reached out toward the pile of loaves. One by one he picked them up and deftly slipped them into his mouth, disregarding the shouts of the trainer.

But once in the water the man decided that he would stay in and drive the elephant out.

"Hi, Jerry," he shouted. "Throw me down the pike. I'll git the blasted critter out o' here if it takes me all night!"

Jerry tossed the short pike pole down onto the shelf and the trainer climbed out to get it. When the elephant saw the pole he immediately began to wade across the quarry hole.

"Oh, no, yuh don't, Toby. I'll git yuh, now," shouted the man, as he plunged back into the water and began to swim toward the beast."

"Git outa here, yuh brute," he thundered, when he came alongside the huge bulk. And he accentuated his command by jabbing the pike deep into the beast's hide. As meekly as a lamb the elephant turned around, after allowing the trainer to climb onto the top of his head, he waded toward the shelf and climbed out of the water without the slightest sign of rebellion.

"There, consarn his pesky hide, he's out now," said the little manager to Bruce, who was still laughing over the comical antics of the big beast.

"Good," said the lad. Then, turning, he called to Babe, "Hi! how about the blasting mat sling— is it finished?"

"Yes, it's ready," shouted the fat Scout.

"Well, then, we're all in good shape," said the patrol leader, inspecting the outfit. "Now for business. Ho, Jiminy, flash Mr. Ford the signal."

Instantly Gordon bounded out of the circle of light and climbed the nearest stone pile. Then with his battery he began to flash the Morse code toward headquarters, where Mr. Ford was waiting. The circus manager took the whole performance in with wide eyes.

"Say, hang it all, you Scouts know a thing or two, don't yuh?"

"Yes, we know enough to be fairly helpful," said Bruce modestly. Then, as he saw Mr. Ford flash back his O. K., he said, "Now we'll let 'er go."

He seized the reverse lever on the motor and threw it over. The derrick drums squeaked a moment before settling down to a business-like grumble. Then the rusted steel cable, with the improvised blasting mat sling dangling at its end, was played out swiftly until the mass of woven rope settled down on the ledge beside the circus men, who were hard at work putting chains about the elephant's feet and trunk so that he could not squirm about in the sling. The adjusting of the heavy affair was no easy task, but the men worked with a will and a few moments later Bruce caught their signal that all was ready.

For a moment he paused with his hand on the starting switch. He was almost afraid to throw it into position. "Oh, if the boom will only hold," he whispered to himself, for to have his plans fail now would have been more than he could endure.

He moved the switch. There was a slight arc as contact was made. Then slowly the motor began to turn. The boom stiffened and creaked ominously as the cable tightened. He pushed the switch over another notch. The big animal was lifted off its feet!

Would the boom hold? Bruce and every member of the troop stood tense and silent, as they saw the big body of the elephant dangling over the pit. He was lifted a foot, two feet, *five* feet! He was snorting and squirming in protest, and Bruce's heart almost stopped when he saw the boom give under his weight.

"Oh, if he would only hold still!" muttered the boy. "He'll smash the timber, sure."

The patrol leader pushed the switch over still another notch and the motor began to hum and sputter. The beast was raised ten feet, fifteen feet, eighteen, twenty. Now he was on the level with the top of the quarry!

Slowly the boom began to work in, creaking and snapping under the strain. Splinters were raising here and there on the timber. Bruce knew it was only a matter of seconds now before the great stick would be shattered. The elephant was but a few feet from safety. Canvas men were reaching out over the quarry's edge to seize the side of the sling. They gripped it! They pulled and tugged, and with a prodigious squeak the boom swung over. Then with a crash it buckled, dropping the elephant on the very brink of the hole!

Fortunately, the timber did not part entirely or some one would have been killed. The lacing of steel derrick cable held it in place, and everything was safe.

It took the Scouts and the circus men a brief

instant to realize this, and when they did a cheer went up that must have waked the villagers in Woodbridge.

The little circus manager was delighted. He rushed up and grasped Bruce's hand:

"Fine work, young feller! Fine work, I say! Now you Scouts all git home and tumble into bed. My men will clean things up here in fine shape. It's half-past three. Sleep 'til ten o'clock and by that time a couple of my best vans will be at that buildin' yuh call headquarters waitin' t' take yuh t' St. Cloud. Yer goin' t' be my guests at t' circus er I'll know the reason why."

"Gee, that's mighty good," said Bruce, excitedly. "How about it, fellows? We don't mind taking *that* sort of pay for a good turn, do we?"

"You bet we don't," shouted the Scouts, enthusiastically. And a few moments later they fell in line and started off toward Woodbridge.

CHAPTER VI

HELPING TO MAKE THE MOVIES

"WHE-E-E-O-O-O! whe-e-e-o-o-o! whe-e-e-o-o-o!" screamed the siren as Bruce Clifford's motorcycle came to a halt in front of the Weir cottage on Willow Street. Then:

"Hi, Bud—Bud-de-de! Hello-o-o, Bud! Come on, wake up!" shouted the leader of the Owl Patrol, cupping his hands about his mouth and directing his voice toward an upstairs window. A moment later the window in question opened and Bud in his undershirt, with a towel in one hand and a cake of soap in the other, appeared.

"What're you making such a row for? I'm awake," he shouted rather irritably, for Bud really never became thoroughly cheerful until after he had had his breakfast.

"Say, Bud, the highway bridge over Muddy Brook—the one just below the railroad tracks on Lake Road, has gone down under a big motor truck full of scenery and things belonging to the Historical Motion Picture Company, the outfit that has been taking Revolutionary War pictures over near Ticonderoga. The machine's half under water and the men need help. There's a chance for the Scouts to get busy. Are you with us?''

"You bet I am. I'll be to headquarters in three winks,'' said the leader of the Blue Heron Patrol, considerably better natured.

"Fine! Hurry now! I'm off to headquarters to call the rest of the fellows together,'' said Bruce, as he started his motorcycle and shot up the long incline that led to the machine-shop headquarters of Quarry Troop No. 1, of Woodbridge, popularly known as the Boy Scout Engineers.

The leader of the Owls had left home a little after daylight that morning with fishing pole and creel strapped to his machine, for he intended trying the brown trout in Concord valley. But when he reached the little highway bridge where the Lake Road crossed a shallow brook near the Rutland Railroad tracks, a situation presented itself that banished all thought of trout fishing.

The ends of the bridge timbers had rotted away from dampness and under the weight of a big motor truck had parted from their stone pier. Their collapse had projected the heavy vehicle front first into the stream, so that its hood was jammed against the abutment, while its hind wheels still remained on the sloping bridge floor. The chauffeur and his two assistants stood surveying the scene in a most dejected attitude.

Of course Bruce stopped at the stream and looked over the situation, asking innumerable questions. But the men were not in a pleasant frame of mind and gave him only disagreeable answers, which nettled the scout to the point of exclaiming:

"Huh, if you weren't so grouchy about it, I'd like to try help you get out of the mess you are in. Maybe we could help a great deal. I'm a member of the Boy Scout Engineers, and it is just our fun to lend a hand in a fix like this."

The chauffeur looked at the lad in amazement for a moment. Then he spoke in milder tones.

"Excuse me, son. I didn't mean t' be so nasty. If you fellows will give us a hand, we'd be mighty much obliged. I know what the scouts are. I've met 'em before.''

"Thank you for the compliment," said Bruce. "We'll be here with block and tackle in less than an hour. In the meantime, get your truck un- loaded," and, turning about, he raced back to town, stopping only to awaken Bud Weir before reach- ing headquarters.

Entering the home of the troop, he hurried to the wire-room on the second floor and began call- ing the scouts from breakfast. The telegraph line leading from headquarters was a big loop that extended through the town and connected with an instrument in the home of every second- class scout, and all the boys could be called to headquarters in a jiffy.

When his summons had been answered by most of the boys, Bruce hurried downstairs and pro- ceeded to get "Old Nanc," the troop's home- made automobile, ready for service. Into it he loaded all the manila rope he could lay hands on, as well as blocks and pulleys, chains, crowbars, axes, sledges and everything else that might come in handy.

By the time this work was well under way the
scouts began to arrive and lend a hand. They
came on motor cycle and on foot until there were
twenty-odd gathered at headquarters. And when
they were all assembled, Bruce outlined briefly the
situation at the Lake Road bridge and gave them
his idea of how the task should be handled. Of
course, they were all eager to undertake the work,
and in a few minutes they were on their way to
the scene of trouble.

The chauffeur and his men had done as Bruce
suggested, and when the lads arrived they found
two great stacks of canvas scenery by the roadside. They gave this only a moment's inspection,
however, for they had work before them. With
as much system as a trained army corps they began to unload the coils of rope and the pulleys.
Then, under Bruce's direction, several wove the
cordage into a block and tackle arrangement.
This done, a group headed by Romper Ryan removed shoes and stockings and began to ford the
shallow stream, carrying the block and tackle with
them. In no time they had one of the pulleys
lashed to a substantial maple tree by the roadside.

The other pulley was fastened to the back end of the automobile truck, which was still on the sloping floor of the bridge.

When this was completed the single strand of rope on which they were to haul was passed back across the stream and attached to the rear axle of "Old Nanc."

Then came the test of the boys' engineering skill. At the request of Bruce the scouts all seized the rope to assist "Old Nanc" in hauling the big machine backward up the grade. Bud, the official driver of the troop's automobile, climbed to his place and everything was ready.

"Now, all together! PULL!" shouted Bruce, and at the command every scout arched his shoulders and hauled his hardest, while "Old Nanc's" engine began to cough and grumble furiously.

The tackle grew taut. The pulleys squeaked and groaned and the bridge timbers protested in like manner as the big truck began to move. Up it crawled, inch by inch. Now the hood was out of water! A moment later the rear wheels were onto the road! Slowly but surely it was lifted out of the brook until, finally, with a mighty tug, the lads backed it clear off the bridge and safely onto the highway.

"Fine!" shouted the chauffeur. "I knew you scouts were the bully boys. But, say, fellows, how's the machine going to get across the stream? We are bound for Woodbridge, you know, and we're on the wrong side of the busted bridge now."

"Oh, maybe we can work that out some way," said Bruce. "I guess we'll try to make a pair of shears out of a couple of fence rails, then hitch the block and tackle to the bridge floor and hoist it back to its proper level again. The rest of the fellows will get all of the discarded railroad ties they can find along the tracks over yonder and build a square crib under the bridge. They can lay the ties on top of each other in log cabin fashion and I guess that will hold up the bridge under your machine. It will make the crossing safe until the town authorities can put new bridge timber in place, too."

"Sounds mighty sensible," said the chauffeur. "Will it take long?"

"I don't think so. It's only half past ten now.

Here comes the ten thirty Montreal Special,'' said Bruce, as the Canadian flyer shot around a bend in the railroad tracks, her whistle screaming her approach to the Woodbridge station.

"Come on, then, let's get busy right away.   Perhaps we can have the machine into Woodbridge by noon,'' said the chauffeur.   Then, to his assistants, he called.   "Hi, you fellows, git over there to the railroad tracks and pick up some o' those old ties.   Go along with the scouts.   They know old ones from new ones.''

All the lads, except two or three of the older boys, waded the brook and started out after crib building material.   The others remained to help Bruce rig up the shears and put the block and tackle into place.

Fortunately, section gangs had been working on the railroad recently, putting in new ties, and there were any number of discarded timbers along the embankment.   These the lads appropriated, for they knew that the railroad men no longer wanted them and that sooner or later a bonfire would be made of them.   The heavy timbers were piled up on the bank of the brook as fast as the scouts could find them, and by the time Bruce and his helpers had hitched the block and tackle to the sagging bridge the crib builders were ready to begin work.

Raising the bridge floor was accomplished quickly, for the wooden structure was nowhere near as heavy as the auto truck. Indeed, "Old Nanc" managed to haul it up all alone. This accomplished, the scouts waded into the water again, and, working in pairs, carried the railroad ties to a point just under the broken structure. The first two ties were put up and down stream and weighted with stones to keep them from floating away. Two more were then placed across the stream on top of the first set, exactly like logs in a cabin. Then, like bees, the boys traveled back and forth to the bank, carrying the heavy ties, until finally the crib was constructed snugly under the bridge flooring with two heavy cross timbers resting safely on top.

When the tackle was finally removed and the bridge platform settled into place and gave every indication of being safely propped up by the crib,

the scouts gave a ringing cheer, for their efforts
had been successful.

And, as if in answer to the cheer, the loud honk-
ing of a motor horn was heard and a big red motor car containing one man and the driver came
tearing down the road.

"Here comes our manager, Mr. Dickle!" exclaimed the chauffeur when he saw the machine.

Mr. Dickle proved to be a very businesslike and
hustling individual. He bounded from the car
before it stopped, demanding at the same time to
know all the particulars of what had happened.
It seems that he had seen the stalled motor truck
from the window of the ten thirty train and had
hired the first automobile he could find at the
Woodbridge station and rushed to the scene of
trouble.

Briefly Bruce and the chauffeur told him all
that had happened and all that had been done.

"Rebuilt the bridge, eh?" Looks as if it would
hold a steam engine now. That's bully," exclaimed Mr. Dickle. "Now, if you fellows can tell
me of a building equipped with electricity that I

can rent for a studio for a couple of days, you will have done me another great favor. We are going to make some historical films of Ethan Allen and the Green Mountain Boys. Say, by the way, you fellows look intelligent. How would you like to be my supes? I'll pay you fifty cents a day. How about it?''

''What's a supe?'' asked Bruce and Bud together.

''Why, a supernumerary. I want a number of people to take part in the production, as Green Mountain Boys or British soldiers or the mob, or rôles like that, where good actors are not needed. I have a big battle scene as a climax. I'll need you in that surely.''

''In the movies, eh? Whoope-e-e-e! Fine!'' exclaimed several, and the manager knew immediately that he would not have to look further for additional members for his cast.

''And, say, about a studio; perhaps you could use the meeting room on the top floor of our headquarters building. We have all the electricity you want, only there isn't much daylight for taking pictures. There are only three windows, and—''

"Tut, tut, never mind the daylight. We don't need it in modern photography. We'll go up and look at the place," said the manager. Then to the chauffeur he shouted: "Here, Jim, fasten a rope to the truck and I'll have this machine of mine tow you up to the scouts' headquarters."

CHAPTER VII

ETHAN ALLEN COMES TO LIFE AGAIN

FOR the next days the troop's headquarters on Otter Hill was the strangest place imaginable. Passers by were surprised to find groups of real Indians in war paint, Colonial soldiers, British troopers and Green Mountain Boys in buckskin garments walking up and down in front of the building or sitting in the sun waiting for their turn to "go on" in the studio room upstairs. These were the regular actors of the Historical Motion Picture Company, who had come to Woodbridge by train to take part in the Ethan Allen film which Mr. Dickle was making.

To be sure, all this fascinated the scouts. It was a decided pleasure to be allowed to circulate among such famous people. Ethan Allen was a big, broad-shouldered actor whose name was known from coast to coast. So was the individual who took the part of Captain Rember Baker, Cap-

tain Warner and Captain Warrington. Anne
Story was a girl whose face the boys had seen on
a dozen different billboards, and there were any
number of other well-known individuals in the
troupe. And there were real live Indians, too,
who afforded the boys no end of interest. Alto-
gether, the advent of the motion picture company
was a liberal education for the lads.

But for knowledge of the technical nature, which
the boys liked best, the interior of headquarters
presented a world of opportunity. When the company's electricians and stage carpenters had finished with their work in the big meeting room
Bruce and his chums scarcely recognized it as the
same place. Two banks of a dozen electric lights
as big as street arc lamps, and just as powerful,
had been strung across the ceiling. These, by
means of reflectors, were made to flood the far end
of the room, "the stage," with a steady white
light.

Behind the light was the camera man, grinding
away steadily, taking sixteen pictures a second,
while before the light were the actors playing
their parts, now in a log cabin, now in a Colonial

mansion and again in a courtroom at Albany, according to the way the scene shifters arranged the portable canvas scenery.

Between the camera man and the actors, to the left of the stage, sat Mr. Dickle in his shirt sleeves, clutching a bundle of manuscript in one hand and a megaphone in the other. Through this effective mouthpiece he directed each of the actors. The members of the cast did their work entirely in pantomime, except when Mr. Dickle bawled a few lines at them, which they repeated so that the camera could register the action of their lips.

It was all so perfectly wonderful to the scouts that they stood for hours watching the making of the film; that is, they stood still and watched while the actors and photographers were at work, but the moment business was suspended, while scenes were changed, they began to ask questions of every one in sight.

They learned that the big lights were a new type of tungsten lamp filled with nitrogen gas which made them burn three times as bright as other lamps. They discovered that the original photographs were only three-quarters of an inch

long and they were magnified from thirty to fifty
thousand times when they were projected onto a
movie screen by the machine in the theater.   They
found out also that raw film cost four cents a
foot, that "movie" actors were paid as high as
$20,000 a year, that there were nearly four hun-
dred American firms making movies, that most
of the films of the world were made in this country, that American "movies" were being shown
in China, Australia, India and all sorts of far-off
corners of the world, and that in one American
city alone the "movie" theaters took in more than
$40,000 a day in admission fees.

All this and a great deal more did the inquisitive youngsters gather, until they became veritable
motion picture encyclopedias. Of course, chief
among the men whom they questioned was Mr.
Dickle. In fact, every time the manager finished
directing a scene, Bruce and several other scouts
pounced upon him and began plying him with
questions concerning the film industry, all of which
he answered in great detail, for he appreciated the
fact that they were boys who wanted to learn and
understand.

It was during one of these periods of catechising that he finally explained the big film he was making at the time.

"This photoplay," he said, "is to be a feature production; five reels of 1,000 feet each. I'm going to give all the details of the troubles Ethan Allen and the Green Mountain Boys had with the authorities of New York State over the New Hampshire Grants. Of course, you boys know the story. It's history."

"You bet we do," said Bruce; "find a Vermont boy who hasn't read about the Green Mountain Boys."

"Well, I'm glad you are so well informed. It will help a little when you take your parts to-morrow afternoon. I've finished the studio work on the film now, and all that remains are some exteriors in the vicinity of the Lake. The film will wind up with a big battle between Allen and his Green Mountain Boys against the Sheriff of Albany, assisted by some Indians and Red Coats."

"I want you fellows to be the original Green Mountain Scouts. Your buckskins are all downstairs in the trunks. They came by express this morning. I'll expect you all to report here to-morrow at two thirty. Get into the duds and come up to the lake. You'll find us all ready for you up there with an automobile full of flintlock rifles and things. The stage will all be set for the big battle around the mouth of the real Ethan Allen cave. How does that suit you?'' It was a thrilling idea.

"How does it suit? Wow; were there ever fellows as lucky as we are? Just think of being in a real movie film; I tell you—''

"Jiminy crickets, we'll have the time of our life, Mr. Dickle. Why, we'll do it for nothing, just for the fun of the thing,'' exclaimed Gordon generously.

"Oh, no, you won't; you'll get fifty cents each, and, besides, I'm paying you ten dollars a day for the use of this building. Forty dollars is due you so far. That should help the troop's treasury a little, eh, boys?''

"You bet it will,'' said Bruce. "Only we don't like—''

"Tut, tut; that'll do. I owe you money, and I'm going to pay it. If you don't take it I'll mail it to your Assistant Scout master, Mr. Ford. I met him yesterday," said Mr. Dickle. Then, to the actors, he called: "Next scene, gentlemen! Ring the bell, Benny!" And Bruce and the scouts realized that it was time for them to leave.

The following day Woodbridge witnessed the strangest scene in its history. It was that of a score of Green Mountain Scouts, in buckskins and coon caps, traveling up the dusty road toward the Lake. Some were astride motor cycles, a half-dozen were crowded into "Old Nanc" and the rest were walking.

An hour after leaving headquarters they reached the lake shore. Ethan Allen's cave was up a very steep grade from the water and the boys could see as they rounded the bend in the road dozens of Red Coats and Indians waiting for them. Bruce and the lads on the motorcycles put on high speed and took the grade in whirlwind fashion but "Old Nanc" was not equal to the hill, so she was parked in a lot by the lakeside and the rest of the troop went up to the cave on foot.

Immediately upon their arrival activities began. Mr. Dickle formed them in line and marched them up beside the big automobile truck that stood in the middle of the road. Here each lad was given a flintlock rifle and sent over to the mouth of the cave, where Ethan Allen and a half-dozen Green Mountain Boys were waiting, seated about a camp fire.

"Now, boys," said the manager, when all had been served with guns and had taken their places, "those weapons of yours are only dummies. I don't want you lads fooling with powder even in a sham battle. I won't be responsible for your eyes. My regular actors will do all the firing necessary, and they will make smoke enough to cover the film. All I want you fellows to do is aim and pull the trigger. Are you ready now, gentlemen? Camera!"

Mr. Dickle stood with his feet apart, megaphone in hand, in the middle of the road. The camera man had set up his tripod on the rear end of the motor truck, which was held on the very brink of the grade by its brakes. At the word "Camera" he began to turn the crank of his machine rapidly, and almost before they knew it the Boy Scout Engineers were being photographed as part of a real feature film.

Action followed swiftly. While the lads were sitting about the fire an Indian came out of the woods. It was Neshobee, the friendly Red Man of Judge Thompson's story. He advanced to Ethan Allen, his hand extended aloft as a sign of friendship. Then he began to talk, pointing into the bushes and up toward the leaves of the trees. Instantly the Green Mountain Boys were alert!

"The Red Coats and the Sheriff!" snapped Allen, and every man was crouching, gun in hand, waiting for the attack. A Red Coat appeared in the bushes!

Up went a dozen muskets, and the next instant there was a thundering roar! The Red Coat disappeared! But others came! They bobbed up everywhere! Behind bushes and trees! From rocks and logs they sprang, advancing and firing in apparently deadly earnestness! The roar of the musketry was deafening! Bruce and his chums were thrilled with enthusiasm, and they snapped their guns at every enemy in sight! On

came the Red Coats and the Indians with the
Sheriff of New York leading them! They advanced into the open, firing deliberately at the little group of defenders about the cave! But their
fire was answered with interest, and soldiers and
Indians were stumbling and falling in all directions!

And above all the din could be heard the voice
of Mr. Dickle, the stage manager, roaring directions through his megaphone. "Great scene!
Fine! Register excitement! Fall down, Murphy!
Tumble over, there, Lisk; you're dead—tumble, I
say. Don't be afraid of your uniform. I'll pay
for that. Fall!—fall!—fall! Now, Green Mountain Boys, up and at 'em! Charge! Charge!
Beat it, you Red Coats—you're licked. Run!
Git! Beat it, I say! After 'em, scouts, after
'em! Fine! Great scene! All right; that'll do.
Quit firing."

The roar of the flintlocks ceased and Bruce and
the rest of the scouts stopped, thoroughly out of
breath with excitement. The Red Coats and Indians stopped also, and, turning about, rejoined
their erstwhile enemies. The "dead" and

"wounded" stood up, too, and began to walk about and chat with the rest, all of which gave the scouts the impression that a "movie" battle was the only really pleasant kind of battle, after all.

"Well, you scouts certainly filled the bill as Green Mountain Boys," said Mr. Dickle when the boys reached the road where he was standing. "That will make a great scene. Now, just as soon as Bob gets his stuff stowed away in the truck, we'll start for town."

Bruce noticed that the camera man was having difficulty in getting his outfit in the truck unassisted, so he ran on ahead of the others to help him.

"Here, Bruce," said the movie operator, "you get up in the wagon and I will hand the things to you and you can stow them under the seat."

The camera man handed up the box-like machine, which Bruce started packing under the seat. Just as the operator started back up the hill to get his tripod, in some unaccountable manner the brakes of the heavy truck loosened and the big vehicle started to roll slowly down the hill. So steep was the grade that the truck gained momentum at a terrific rate.

Bob, the camera man, noticing what had happened, turned and ran swiftly down the hill. But it had gained such headway that he couldn't overtake it.

"Hi, there!" shrieked Mr. Dickle. "Stop that truck! Stop it! My film! It's all in the camera, and the truck's running away! Stop it, some one! Save the film!"

Bruce's first impulse was to jump from the truck and leave it to its fate, but when he heard the manager's frantic appeal to save the precious film he climbed quickly over the back of the high seat. In another instant he grasped the steering wheel and jammed his foot down upon the brake lever.

Then bang—! the brake band snapped and the truck lurched forward again! Bruce had applied the brake too suddenly, and the next moment he found himself in a runaway motor truck that could not be stopped until it reached level ground.

The patrol leader felt like he was turning cold. Before him stretched a long grade, and at the end a sharp turn! If he did not make that turn the motor truck would crash against a rock or tree and kill him, or at best it would plunge into the Lake and then the film would be lost! Could he make the turn?

On rushed the massive truck. It had developed express train speed now and it rocked from side to side like a ship in a gale as it tore down the rough country road! Bruce clutched the big steering wheel with deathlike grip and tried his mightiest to keep the cumbersome vehicle straight! He realized that a loose stone or a deep rut meant death to him and destruction to the motor car! His teeth were clenched and his face was white! The wind had whisked away his coonskin cap.

"Oh, if I can only make that turn! I must! I've *got* to!" he told himself, as he saw the distance to the foot of the hill being eaten up by the flying motor car. Nearer and nearer came the turn. It was a hundred yards away. Now seventy, fifty, forty! Would the truck stay on all four wheels or would it go plunging on madly, end over end, into the lake? Could he make it? The road bent slightly now. Bruce followed the curve.

Now came the turn. Bruce tugged at the wheel. The big truck swerved. It was skidding! It was on two wheels and ploughing up the dust in great clouds! It was almost around! It was around! The road ahead of him was straight and clear!

Bruce breathed a great sigh of relief. And so did fifty individuals who had been watching the terrible race from the top of the hill. They cheered loud and long when the big truck shot safely around the bend and headed up the level road toward Woodbridge. Then all of them started down the grade pell mell, nor did they stop until they reached the place where the truck had finally stalled. Then every one tried to shake the boy's hand.

"By Jove, but for your nerve, Bruce, my boy, we'd have been minus film and motor truck. For pure grit, I think you scouts take the prize. I wish I could think of some way to repay you," cried Mr. Dickle, pumping Bruce around somewhat roughly.

"Why—er—you see—we don't want any pay for what we do, but if it can be arranged, I—I— well, we sure would like to see that 'movie.' Can't you send one to the Woodbridge Theater?" said Bruce.

"Huh, send one to the Woodbridge Theater! Why, I'll bring the first release of it to Woodbridge myself and show it in your headquarters. How'll that suit you fellows?"

And the enthusiastic replies of the scouts convinced the "movie" manager that he had hit the right idea.

CHAPTER VIII

THE PRIZE CONTEST

"WELL, fellows, there's this much about it, if we are going to build a real sure enough motorboat this year we've got to get a hustle on us and earn some money. With the rent we received from the Historical Motion Picture Company and the money we secured from the circus ticket wagon we have just $73.75. We need $94.00 to buy the motor alone, even with the reduction that Mr. Clifford can get for us. And added to that is the expense of extra lumber and fittings, which will be at least thirty dollars more. Now where do we stand, I'd like to know?"

Thus did Bud Weir unburden his mind to the other boys of the Quarry Troop, sometimes called, because of their mechanical skill, the Boy Scout Engineers.

All spring the scouts had been planning to build

a motorboat to be used on Long Lake. They had had their summer camp on the shores of this lake for the past two years, and they intended to have a camp there as usual this year, but they had decided to make it a construction camp and spend most of their time building a thirty-foot power boat, which would be the largest vessel on the lake. The idea was to increase the troop's fund in the treasury as much as possible during the Winter and Spring and use the money to purchase a three-horsepower gasoline motor, which they calculated would be large enough to drive the boat faster than any craft thereabout.

But somehow the months had hurried past and the fund had not increased at a proportionate pace. Indeed if it had not been for a windfall of forty odd dollars from the Historical Motion Picture Company, the treasury would have been in a very bad way. The scouts really could not understand it at all. They had worked hard, or at least they thought they had, and they had contributed every cent they had made toward the engine fund, but somehow the balance in the Woodbridge bank looked mighty small to the scouts.

"What the dickens is the matter with us anyway, are we lazy?" queried Nipper Knapp, breaking the long silence that followed Bud's remark.

"By jiminy, it looks that way to me," said Jiminy Gordon emphatically.

"It's procrastination that—"

"Whoops! Hi! what was that word? Ho, ho, say it again, Bruce," shouted Romper Ryan hilariously.

"He's worked for months on that *Boys' Life Dictionary Contest*," said Ray Martin, "that's what's the matter with Bruce. What does it mean? Maybe it's something to eat!"

"Aw, say, quit your joshin' me," said Bruce, "that's a real word. It means—ah—er—well—"

"Sure it does, we knew it all the time, didn't we, Romper?" said Nipper Knapp.

"That's exactly what it means," said Bud quite soberly.

"Well, it means that we've been putting off work. We haven't come down to brass tacks. And now we're up against it and our motorboat proposition falls through," snapped Bruce.

"Well, if that's what it means then you told the

truth,'' said Bud, resuming his indignant attitude; "we fellows haven't been on the job. I haven't made a cent in three weeks and neither has any one of the rest of you. Now be honest, have you?"

"No, we haven't," said Dug Maston.

"I guess we are actually growing lazy," said Romper solemnly.

Then Babe Wilson, the sarcastic fat scout, added:

"No, we haven't been lazy, we've just been waiting for opportunity to knock at our door—''

(*Rap—rap—rap, rap—rap—rap—rap.*)

Babe looked startled and swallowed hard. Then, his sense of humor bobbing to the surface again, he grinned.

"That's Mr. Opportunity," he said.

"No, it wasn't," said Romper, rushing to the window, "it was a blasted old bill poster tacking a sign on Headquarters— Hi! git out o' there! This isn't an old barn!" he shouted to the bill poster.

But that individual never heard him and kept tacking away until the bill was up. Then he went on down the road whistling merrily.

"Hang it, Headquarters will look like a bill-board soon. I'm going down to pull his blooming old sign off our wall," said Romper, as he disappeared through the doorway and stamped down the stairs. But a few moments later he seemed to have changed his mind, for he was heard to shout:

"Hi, fellows, come on down. It's worth reading anyway." And what the scouts read when they crowded about him was:

$200   In Prizes   **$200**
for
Brown Tail Moth Exterminators

The Town of Woodbridge is offering $200 in prizes to the individuals who can advance and demonstrate a practical method of exterminating the Brown Tail Moths that are infesting the trees in the township. For particulars apply to Mayor's Office, Town Hall.

Three Prizes Offered
$100   **$60**   **$40**

"Say, was that opportunity, after all?" asked Babe in wide-eyed amazement when he read the poster.

And every boy looked at every other boy and wondered.

If there are any who do not believe that boys can become genuinely interested in study, they should have visited the Quarry Troop headquarters a few days after the discovery of the work of the bill poster. For at least three consecutive afternoons a dozen lads spent their time in the big meeting room on the second floor poring over dry looking pamphlets which bore the stamp of the Bureau of Entomology of the United States Department of Agriculture.

They were all perusing this literature with the one purpose—to learn as much as they could about the habits of the brown tail moths, for they hoped in their study to discover some new and original way to exterminate the pest and thereby win one of the three generous prizes offered by the town authorities. But though they pursued the subject relentlessly none of them seemed able to generate an idea that smacked of originality.

"Aw, say, fellows, this will never do," said Babe Wilson. "We can't compete in this contest. We don't know anything about chemistry or things like that. Why, we don't even know a Brown Tail moth when we see one." He disconsolately tossed away his pamphlet and shoved his hands into his pockets.

"Pshaw, don't give up so soon," said Bud Weir. "This reading isn't very gay but all the same we are learning some things we should know. And even if we are not familiar with chemistry, we may be able to figure out a way of getting rid of them by means of some mechanical appliance."

"I think this is mighty interesting," said Bruce, looking up from his leaflet. "I know now what's ailing those apple trees down back of our barn. The Brown Tail moths are in them. Listen to this: 'The principal injury caused by these moths is due to the feeding habits of the larvæ. They attack apple, pear, plum, oak, elm and willow trees. If the infestation is bad the caterpillars are often numerous enough to devour the leaves as fast as the trees are able to develop them. As the webs are made on the terminals the growth of the tree is frequently checked.'

"Those apple trees of ours haven't had a full grown leaf on them this Spring and there are webs in the tops of them, too. That's the work of Brown Tails all right."

"The most interesting thing to me about these little codgers is the way they got here," said Romper Ryan. "They came from Europe about 1897, so this book says. Came over on some young trees imported here. There couldn't have been more than a couple of cocoons, but look how they have spread since that time. They were first seen in Somerville, Massachusetts, but now they are all over the New England States. They are only just getting into Vermont, though."

"This pamphlet says that the female moth flies a great distance," said Jiminy Gordon, growing enthusiastic about the subject, "and that the female Gipsy moth, which is another kind of pest, can't fly at all. By jiminy, I thought all moths could fly, didn't you? It also says that the female Brown Tail moth is attracted by strong lights and can be found fluttering around arc lamps almost any warm—"

"Does it? Where? Where does it say they like strong light?" exclaimed Nipper Knapp.

"Why, what the dickens struck you? It says so right here. Just listen: 'These moths are attracted to strong light such as electric arc lights, and as they fly at night it is often possible to secure many specimens around arc lamps in cities and towns during the latter part of June and the first half of July. The—' "

"Whoop! That solves it! I got it, fellows! It's as easy as rolling off a log. We win the $100 prize sure!" exclaimed Nipper Knapp excitedly. Then while the boys were looking at him in utter amazement he continued.

"Listen, fellows! I was running mother's electric vacuum cleaner this morning before I started to school. I saw how easily the motor-driven fan sucked in everything in sight. I held the nozzle near a fly on the window pane and *zipp—p-p,* in went Mr. Fly. I thought right away that a big vacuum cleaner would make a fine moth catcher if we could only get near enough to the moths. And I even figured out a plan for a large one which wouldn't cost very much and could be made mostly of wood. But I knew it was foolish 'cause we couldn't get near the moths. Then—"

"Great! I see your plan. You are going to attract your moths by a light and then catch 'em with the suction cleaner," exclaimed Bruce.

"Sure, and here's how I'm going to do it.   I'm going to take one of the automobile's searchlights and shine it off on to some trees and then put the vacuum cleaner just under the light beams.   Then, when Mr. Moth comes flying down the path of light and gets over the top of the sucker—*zing*, in he goes.   Get my idea?   Wait, I'll draw a plan of the thing for you,'' and, rushing over to the writing table in the corner, Nipper began to draw hastily while the scouts all crowded around him and watched.

"There you are.   There's the whole plan of the thing.   Easy to make and easy to operate and I guess it's original all right."

The drawings traveled from hand to hand, each lad scrutinizing them carefully for some fault in the mechanical detail.

"Jiminy, I think you've struck it," exclaimed Gordon.

"Struck it?   Why, man, he's got the first prize in his pocket right now," insisted Romper as he looked over the plans.

"Well, if it meets with your approval, fellows, let's get busy right now and build our moth trap."

"Right-o. No more procras—something-or-other, as Bruce said the other day. We'll get busy immediately," said Bud Weir.

"Well, first of all I think we should talk it over with Mr. Ford. He will be able to see flaws in our plans where we can't, you know," said Nipper.

"That was exactly my idea. And, by the way, did you notice that the pamphlet from the Mayor's office named Mr. Ford among the members of the judging committee in this contest?" said Bruce.

"Yes, I did," said Bud, "and for that reason I think he would like to see us boys try for the prize even though we don't win anything. Come on, we'll go over and talk with him."

Bud was quite right. When Mr. Ford learned that the boys had become interested in the fight against the Brown Tail moth he was delighted.

"That's the stuff, scouts. Take an interest in everything in the nature of a public improvement. If you grow up with that idea in mind you will make useful citizens," he said, when the boys informed him that they had been studying the Brown Tail moth campaign and intended to try for one of the town's prizes.

"Well, I'm afraid that it was more of a selfish motive that led us to take an interest. The troop needs one of those prizes to swell its treasury," said Bruce.

"Never mind, many of the noblest works in this world resulted from the selfish desire on the part of some one who wanted to win *some* kind of a prize. But I won't sermonize. Let me see what you have in mind as a moth exterminator," said the Assistant Scoutmaster.

The electrical engineer spent nearly half an hour in silent contemplation of Nipper's drawings after the plan had been explained to him. Finally, his eyes sparkling with amusement, he laid the drawings onto his desk and remarked:

"By Jove, you fellows are about the keenest observers I've met in some time. It all grew out of watching a vacuum cleaner, eh? Well, well, well, I think that idea is remarkable. I'm certain it will work. You should have it patented immediately. Make another set of drawings for me, Nipper, and I'll send them down to my patent attorney in Washington. Perhaps you may have struck it richer than you expect. You may be able to put the device on the market. Who knows? In the meantime get busy and build one and let me see how it works.''

"We are going down and buy the material right away," said Bruce, enthusiastically, "and father says he will have the suction fan made over in his shop. It can be built of sheet iron and won't cost much, you know."

"All right, go ahead. I'll come over to headquarters now and then and watch you work," said Mr. Ford.

CHAPTER IX

WORKING TO WIN

NOT since the days preceding the Firemen's Tournament when the motorcycle fire department was being outfitted had the scout engineers been busier than they were the following few weeks. Every afternoon after the academy let out, and every evening they could spare from their studies was devoted to the construction of the moth trap. They worked with snap and vim, for upon the success of their product depended the possibility of a troop motorboat.

And it was well that they had this enthusiasm, for a time limit had been set on the contest. According to the information received from the Mayor's office the contest would close the last Monday in June and the five days following would be devoted to testing the various methods and appliances entered. With the assistance of Mr. Ford the lads had already made their entry, sending

drawings and details of their device to the committee of judges.   But in spite of their fast work
it was apparent that they would not complete
their contrivance until the middle or latter part of
the week set for the test.

They were determined that $100 of the $200 offered by the town should be added to the troop's
account in the Woodbridge bank, however, and
when scouts take that attitude in any matter one
can rest assured of a period of industry.   They
worked like beavers and the *rap, rap, rap* of hammers, the *buzz-z-z* of band and jigsaws and the
hum-m of motors could be heard in their workshop on the first floor of the headquarters building
at almost any hour.

Of course, the boys were not entirely sure that
they would win first or even third prize, because
there were any number of others competing for
the same honors.   Indeed, farmers and even business men in and around Woodbridge were experi-
menting with chemical exterminators and various
other ingenious devices and all of these would
have an equal chance with the appliance invented
by the boys.   But the lads were sportsmen enough

to take their chances with the rest.   Indeed, they even went so far as to stake some of the precious motor money on the result, for they took fifteen dollars from the Woodbridge bank to pay for the lumber and other material needed to build Nipper's big vacuum pest catcher.

"If we don't win that prize now all our chances for a motorboat are gone for sure," said Babe Wilson when Bud Weir announced the withdrawal of part of the fund.

"Well, that isn't the way to look at it.   Just say we are *going* to win the prize and then get busy and work for it," insisted Bud, trying to instil confidence in the stout scout.

Day by day the neatly finished boards grew to represent Nipper's idea of a moth exterminator. And finally, after what seemed to the boys an unusually long time, the suction fan arrived from Bruce's father's mill.   It was already attached to a one-quarter horsepower electric motor, for Mr. Clifford knew that none of the motors in the scouts' workshop were small enough to be used on a fan with six-inch blades.   By this time the lads had all but finished the big wooden trumpet and it was only necessary to set the fan, bolt the motor into place and give the whole thing a coat of paint.

But already the last Monday of the month had passed and only a day or two remained in which the boys could test their machine before the judges. Day and night since the beginning of the week contestants had been claiming the attention of the judges with their schemes for extermination. Most of these had been tried out and many were said to be very successful. On one or two occasions the scouts had gone out to look over these tests, but to their mind none of them looked as effective as the moth trap they were building.

On Thursday night Mr. Ford visited headquarters looking rather anxious, for he had heard very little from the boys during the last few days and he was afraid they were not going to put their machine together in time to appear before the judging committee with it. He was greatly relieved to find that the lads were about to put the motor and fan in place and he realized that this marked almost the last stage of their work.

"Well, boys, it looks all right to me," he said.

"When are you going to be ready for the official tryout?"

"Just as soon as we can put the automobile lamp into place. We are building some iron brackets for that now. We'll be all ready by to-morrow evening, I guess. That will give us one full day leeway. The tests can be conducted up to midnight Saturday, can't they?"

"Sure, I'll see that the judges are ready for you. I have an engagement that may keep me a little bit late, but I'll get there. Where are you going to test it?"

"Out on the back road here; down by the bend opposite Chipman's Hill," said Nipper.

"Fine, I'll be there. Say, by the way, I was talking about your idea down town this evening and a reporter from the *Journal* heard me. He seemed very much interested when I told him about your work and he wants to come up and see the machine. He'll probably be up some time to-morrow. Perhaps I can get him up to see the test. If I can I— Listen, is that some one coming? Sure enough, perhaps it is he. Open the door, Bruce."

Bruce swung open the big double door and Rogan, one of the reporters for the Woodbridge *Journal* and the local correspondent for the St. Cloud *Call*, entered.

"Hello, boys," he shouted good naturedly. "Heard you have a new wrinkle in moth catchers. Is that the machine? Looks mighty businesslike. Is it ready to test? Well, if there isn't Mr. Ford. How are you? What do you think of the scout's invention? How does it work? Whose idea is it. Where—?"

"Oh, goodness gracious, don't ask 'em so fast," said Bruce. "We'll answer them one at a time and explain the machine to you if you'll give us a chance."

"Sure. Excuse me. Go right ahead," said Rogan, his inquisitive blue eyes taking in everything in the room.

Nipper had the honor of describing his own invention, which he did with no little pride. And evidently Rogan was impressed for, after cross-examining Mr. Ford and going into the device from every angle, he wrote a two-column story which appeared on the first page of the *Journal* the following morning. Also he telephoned a story to the St. Cloud paper which the boys read the following afternoon.

As soon as the Academy closed the next day the scouts hurried to headquarters, for they had a great deal to do before they could carry out the test that evening. Two or three attended to the work of removing one of the searchlights from "Old Nanc" and putting it into place on top of the moth catcher, while the rest of the boys strung a temporary line of wire from the headquarters' switchboard to a point about two hundred yards up the road. They intended to conduct the test there and throw the searchlight into the trees on Chipman Hill across the valley.

It was dinner time when the wires were in place and the scouts, after a last look about, all went home to get something to eat and to wait the coming of darkness.

They began to return to headquarters about half past seven. Bruce, Nipper Knapp, and Ray Martin were the first to arrive and, to their surprise, they found at least two dozen people waiting outside of headquarters.

"Well, what does this mean?" inquired Bruce of Nipper.

"Well, I guess they read Rogan's story in the *Journal*. He said we were going to have a test to-night, you know."

"Then we're going to have a gallery of spectators! Oh, well, we don't mind, do we, boys?"

"You bet we don't—if the thing will only work," said Nipper.

Soon, other scouts arrived and presently an automobile rolled up to the door and four of the town's councilmen climbed out. The party was composed of Mr. Bassett, Mr. Bates, Mr. Adams and Mr. Franklin, all members of the Mayor's committee of judges. The lads were disappointed not to see Mr. Ford among them, but they felt confident that he would appear in time for the official test.

The Councilmen looked over the moth trap with critical eyes and asked innumerable questions. Then finally Mr. Bassett, chairman of the committee, spoke.

"Well, Scouts, it surely looks like a good plan.

but will it catch 'em, that's what we want to know?''

"We are not certain of that ourselves, sir, but we'll take it out and test it. Then we'll surely know,'' said Nipper. In a few moments the moth catcher had been loaded into "Old Nanc" and the scouts, judges and about one hundred townfolk who had gathered to see the demonstration, started up Otter Creek road. By the time the boys had loaded the moth catcher into "Old Nanc" the entire troop was there.

Twilight had gone and the stars were coming out when "Old Nanc" arrived at the appointed location. Every one was extremely curious and the moment the moth catcher was put on the ground men and women alike began to inspect the contrivance closely. It was fully twenty minutes before the boys could connect the wires to the searchlight and the motor. Then a scout was sent post haste back to headquarters to throw the switch and let the current into the new line.

When this was done Nipper, who was in charge on this occasion, took his place beside the contrivance. Scouts with staffs were detailed to keep the small crowd back and away from the front of the machine.

"Are you all ready, Nipper?" said Bruce.

"Sure," said Nipper. Then, "say, is Mr. Ford here? I wish he was; I'd like to have him see this. Oh, Bruce, if it will only work! I'm getting as nervous as a cat." He glanced toward the automobile where the four judges sat waiting.

"Tut, tut, don't get fussed," said Bruce, trying hard to conceal his own suppressed excitement.

"All right, here goes," said Nipper as he turned the lamp switch, and a moment later the motor switch.

Instantly a long arm of light reached out across the valley and focused on the heavy growth of elm trees on the opposite hill side. The motor began to hum and the fan to buzz loudly. Every one was attention. Every eye was riveted in the long shaft of light that stretched forth into the night. A minute they waited, two minutes, five minutes! Nothing happened!

"Oh—this suspense is terrible," groaned Nipper.

"You're right, it is," whispered Bruce.

Every scout felt the same way. Was it a failure? Was their idea only visionary, after all? Oh, why didn't something happen to relieve the tension. Why didn't—

"Look! There's a moth," said some one.

"Where?" asked half a dozen breathlessly.

"Out there! Look! Can't you see him?" said others.

Sure enough, coming down the long pathway of light was a solitary moth winging its fitful way toward the lamp. Now it was in the light and now it dodged out into the darkness. But always it returned a few feet nearer to the waiting scouts. It seemed irresistibly drawn toward the auto lamp.

"Come on, come a little closer and we'll have you," whispered Nipper excitedly.

On it came toward the upturned mouth of the vacuum. It was ten feet away, then eight, seven, six. Now it felt the air disturbance, for it began to flutter harder. Then—*zipp!*

It was caught in the air current and in a twinkle disappeared down the yawning mouth of the sucker.

A mighty cheer went up. But they were silenced quickly when another moth appeared. But before this one had gone half way down the light shaft, two others came. Then came two more, then three or four, until they were fluttering in the white light like so many scraps of paper. And always when they reached a point over the opening of the sucker they were whisked out of sight like a flash, to be carried into the big bag at the other end of the machine.

The crowd began to press in closer. The men were talking loudly now and congratulating the young engineers, and as for Nipper and his comrades, well, they were pleased, and showed it by the smiles they wore.

But just at this moment the sound of an automobile coming from the direction of headquarters was heard and the next instant Mr. Ford's car dashed up.

"Hello, boys, how's she working?" he inquired and there was something in the tone of his voice that disturbed the scouts.

"Why, it's running in great shape. We have nearly half a bag full of moths now. What's the matter?" queried Nipper.

"Well, I have some bad news for you. I'm sorry, fellows, but your little machine isn't as original as we thought it was. Here's a telegram I received this evening from my attorneys in Washington. They say that a machine like yours was invented in Germany several years ago and patented in this country, too. They say several stories were printed about it in German and American magazines at the time. That means that we can't put it on the market as we had visions of doing and—!"

"Well, well, that's too bad," said deep-voiced Mr. Bassett, who had come out of the automobile with the other judges to hear what Mr. Ford had to say. "Too bad they can't get a patent on it. I thought the lads had an A-1 business proposition here and I was about to make 'em a spot cash offer for an interest in it. Why, it's the best thing we've seen in all the tests. No one has had anything anywhere near as good."

"But—but—you don't mean we can't win the contest," stammered Nipper nervously, looking at Mr. Bassett.

"Win! Win! Why, lads, you've won in a

walk. Hasn't he, gentlemen? We haven't seen anything as good as this, have we?"

"We certainly have not," said Mr. Adams. "Of course, the boys win. They get the $100 prize, but that's a mighty small amount for such ingenuity. If it wasn't for that German inventor you could have made thousands of dollars out—"

"Pshaw, we only wanted first prize," exclaimed Nipper Knapp. Then he shouted, "Hi, fellows, we win, and we'll have our motorboat. Whoope-e-e-e! Three cheers." And all, including the men, joined in: "Hip—hip—hoo-ray!" the noise of which didn't bother the moths in the least as they kept on fluttering toward the light and disappearing into the trap.

CHAPTER X

THE BOY FROM ARIZONA

"SAY, fellows, I have the idea we—"

"Jiminy!" interrupted Jiminy Gordon. "Romper's got an idea—first he ever had in his life. Come, spit it out, and if it isn't any better than the rest we've been listening to, we'll maul you—won't we, fellows?"

"Bet we will," said Bud Weir.

"We'll duck him in the creek," threatened Nipper Knapp.

"Come on there, young man, let us know what's in your cranium. None of the rest of us has been able to get even the glimmer of an intelligent suggestion," said Bruce Clifford.

"Well, here it is," said Romper, getting to his feet. "We'll furnish a climax to our part of the Fourth of July celebration by presenting Woodbridge with a city flag—we'll make the suggestion, get it approved by the village council, have old Granny Mastin make it and pres—"

"Hi, hi, not so fast—you're rushing along like a train of cars—trying to dodge that ducking, aren't you? Now, slower—what's this idea? What do you mean by a city flag? Never heard of such a thing before," said Ray Martin.

"Huh, you haven't? Well, you're a fine scout. Don't you ever read the papers?" said Romper with disgust.

"I've heard of it," interrupted Bruce, "and it's a bully suggestion. A number of American cities have flags—a distinctive ensign, just like patrol flags that we scouts have. New York has just adopted one, and I can't see why Woodbridge shouldn't have a flag of her own. Romper's idea is a corker. We can suggest a flag and get the approval of the Woodbridge council. Then on the Fourth we can present it to the city and have a grand old celebration. Romper deserves a vote of thanks instead of a ducking."

In truth, Romper had piloted Quarry Troop out of a most trying dilemma. Here is how matters stood before he suddenly became inspired: Woodbridge had been planning a safe and sane Fourth of July celebration, with a pageant, municipal night fireworks and various other forms of a good time. All of which was to take place at the Firemen's Tournament Field on the outskirts of the town. Quarry Troop had been invited to give an exhibition.

So far as that was concerned, the boys were ready and willing to give exhibitions in almost any of the many branches of scouting at a moment's notice, for they were all well trained. But the fact that the occasion was Independence Day and that there would be hundreds of strangers watching them made the lads eager to give an extra good performance and end with a grand flourish— something spectacular.

Now, just what this climax was to be required deep thought, and half a dozen of the older scouts of the troop had gathered under the big maple in front of their machine-shop headquarters on Otter Creek hill to ponder the situation. They had been sprawled in various attitudes in the shade of the old tree for more than half an hour, each one doing his utmost to think of something original. All kinds of suggestions were advanced, but none

was worth considering until Romper finally stirred
up his flag idea.

It did not take the wide-awake youngsters long
to comprehend the spectacular element in this
proposition, however, and presently they were talking away at a furious rate, planning the details.

"Look here, why not make the order of events
like this," said Bruce. "First we'll pitch a real
scout camp and then put up our wireless outfit,
just as we had decided. Beforehand we'll erect
a big pole and a little pole to hold the aerial.
'Old Nanc' can carry the outfit we have on the
headquarters roof to Firemen's Field and we can
borrow one of the batteries from Dad's electric
truck and take that along to furnish our current.

"Then, after the wireless is up and working,
we can wind up the performance by presenting the
town with a flag. That should make a real hit,
eh, fellows? We'll get Mr. Ford to make a speech
from the reviewing stand and then, after the
Mayor has answered, we'll raise the flag on the
big aerial pole and salute it. How do you like
that for a programme?"

"Great," exclamed several of the scouts.

"Bully," said Bud.

"Best ever," asserted Nipper Knapp. "But say, here we've been talking about giving the town a flag, now what's it to look like?"

"Jove, that's right," said Ray Martin. "What sort of a flag is it to be? Let's make it green and purple, green to signify—ah—"

"Yes, let's add pink, canary and sky blue," interrupted sarcastic Babe Wilson, "what do you think this is going to be, a rainbow?"

"Well, I think we should talk the plan over with Mr. Ford and let him give our suggestion to the City Councilmen. They may have some ideas as to what the Woodbridge flag should look like," said Bruce.

"Sure," said Ray.

"All right, I'll—"

"Say, fellows," interrupted Romper in a whisper, while he watched a solitary figure coming up the road, "here comes that chap we had at headquarters yesterday, Dick what's-his-name?"

"Sure enough," said Bud Weir. "Say, come

on fellows, let's go inside; we don't want a 'fraid cat like him hanging around with us.''

"Aw, say, that isn't right," replied Bruce in an undertone. "Don't snub a fellow like that. I think it was sort of childish for him to be afraid, but he looks like a pretty good chap, at that."

But the lad in question evidently did not intend to "hang around." Instead he made his way up Otter Creek hill, passed the group in front of headquarters with a nod and a cheerful "howdy" and continued on his way. He was a short, thickset youngster of about sixteen and he walked with a peculiar stride, for his legs were slightly bowed.

Dick Austin was his name and he had come from his home in Arizona to spend his Summer vacation with an aunt in Woodbridge.

Several of the scouts had met him at various places in the village since he had been in town, and had tried to make his acquaintance, but he seemed to keep to himself a great deal. The day before the Fourth of July conference under the maple, however, two of the lads had encountered him on the street, and out of pure kindness of heart had invited him to accompany them to head-quarters.

But much to their surprise Dick did not like the machine shop at all. He objected to the hum of motors and he jumped every time he saw the flashes from the wireless spark gap. He refused to try a ride on the tandem seat of one of the troop's motorcycles, and when he received a slight shock after several of the boys had persuaded him to take hold of the handles of a static electric ma-chine, he became thoroughly frightened.

"Look year," he said with a decided southern accent, "I don't like this year 'lectric business no how. Hit's dangerous stuff an' I'm afeard o' hit. Yo' see I hain't been used t' hit down whar I lived an' I cain't feel comfortable with a lot of machinery so close to me. No, sirree, I'd rather leg it out o' here and git into t' open."

Whereupon he left headquarters without wait-ing to listen to the scouts, who tried to explain that it was only high-tension electricity that was not at all dangerous and that there was no current of that nature at headquarters.

Dick's attitude had quite surprised the Quarry

Scouts. How a normal boy could fail to be interested in machinery, know nothing about electricity, and actually refuse to ride on a motorcycle because the throbbing engine scared him, was more than they could understand. They quickly decided that he was a coward and had already lost respect for him, as was evident from the caustic comments made by the group under the maple after he had passed.

"Huh," said Ray Martin, "just imagine a fellow getting fidgety over a motor; regular girl."

"It does seem queer," said Bruce. Then getting to his feet and brushing the dust from his trousers he continued:

"Say, fellows, if we are going to try this flag stunt I think it's up to us to get a wiggle on. We've only two weeks to do the work in, you know. I'm going to see Mr. Ford now and talk it over with him. Who wants to go along?"

"I'll go," said Bud Weir.

"So'll I," added Romper.

"All right, come along," replied Bruce. And five minutes later three motorcycles were scooting out toward the hydro-electric plant where Mr.

Ford, the Quarry Troop's Assistant Scoutmaster, was superintendent.

Two days later three lads in scout uniforms were to be seen in the ante-room of the Council Chamber in the Woodbridge Town Hall. They composed the Flag Committee of the Quarry Troop and as they sat there in the straight-backed chairs they looked to be the most uncomfortable trio in all the State of Vermont.

And they were uncomfortable. You see, Bruce, Bud and Romper were waiting patiently the decision of the Councilmen, who were convening behind the closed doors of the room to their left. It was the occasion of the regular weekly meeting of the body, but the fact that the town fathers were debating the adoption of a town flag made the session the most important in the history of Woodbridge, so far as the three scouts were concerned.

"Huh, we've been sitting here just fifteen minutes; seems like fifteen hours," said Bruce in a husky whisper. His eyes were on the big regulator clock that ticked away solemnly on the wall across the room.

As for Bud and Romper, they remained silent, gazing nervously out the window. A little later Romper said: "Maybe they're going to turn us down and—"

He was interrupted by the opening of the swinging doors that led to the Council Chamber. Mr. Bennet, Mayor Worthington's secretary, appeared.

"Scouts," he said, saluting, "the Mayor would like the pleasure of your presence in the Council Room."

It required every ounce of self-control the scouts could summon to walk into that sanctum. How they managed to travel the space from one room to the other without stumbling over rugs or doorsills will ever be a mystery to them.

Presently, however, they found themselves at the lower end of the long mahogany table at which the nine officials were seated. At the head was the dignified Mayor, while to the right and left were ranged the councilmen, all of whom the boys recognized when finally they became more accustomed to the surroundings.

"Scouts," said the Mayor, and at the sound of

his voice each lad saluted, "we have considered your plan to present the town of Woodbridge with a flag, and we have unanimously voted it an excellent idea. Moreover, lads, we have adopted the design and colors of the proposed emblem."

This good news helped to dispel the scouts' nervousness. They were too attentive now to think of being timid.

"We have decided," continued Mr. Worthingington, "that the design shall be a blood red flag with a city seal in the center of it. It shall be red because that is the color that signifies strength, fire, virility, and all that is healthy and normal. And we shall follow the lead of other cities and have an official seal of the community; for the seal, we have decided on the pine tree of Vermont in the upper portion and a quarry derrick, signifying the marble industry of Woodbridge, below. How do you like that, boys?"

"Wonderful," exclaimed the three lads in unison.

"Glad to hear it. Now good luck to you and I hope our Fourth of July celebration is a big success," said the town's chief, dismissing them with a bow.

The scouts were all smiles as they descended the broad steps of the town hall and started down the gravel path to the street, where they had left their motorcycles.

"Jove, we'll have some celebration, eh, fellows?" said Romper.

"You bet we will," assured Bud.

"Yes, but we have a lot of work to do yet before everything will be ready," stated Bruce. "We'll go over to Granny Mastin's right away and find out if she'll make the flag for us. We'll get Nipper to drawn a design for her. Then we'll have to come back and get the silk and whatever else she wants to do the work with. And say, fellows, we'll have to erect our poles at Firemen's Field, do you realize that? We'll be mighty busy for a while—hello, look who's inspecting our motorcycles."

Bud and Romper looked up in time to see Dick Austin, the boy from Arizona, scrutinizing the three machines that were lined up at the curb.

"Howdy," he said as they came up. "I was just eyeing these here critters. Look blamed ferocious, they do."

"Would you like to ride on the tandem behind me?" asked Bruce.

"Who, me?" exclaimed Dick. "No, sirree, yo' cain't git me to straddle that there animal. Ef 'twas a hoss I'd be tickled to death, but you cain't git a snorting machine under me."

"Huh," said Bud, contemptuously, when Dick was out of earshot, "that sounds like a bluff to me. Bet he's afraid of a horse, too."

"Oh, I don't know," said Bruce, as he started his engine, "he has the legs of a horseman and he comes from Arizona, you know."

"Yes, but he's a scared cat," asserted Romper as the trip got under way.

CHAPTER XI

THE COURAGE OF A COWARD

WOODBRIDGE was a profusion of bunting and streamers on Independence Day. Almost every building, from the meanest little stores on Stone Street to the big business blocks on Willow and State Streets, was gay with flags and emblems. The thoroughfares were thronged with people, too. Summer folk from the cities, mingled with the easily distinguished farmers who had come to town for the celebration, and these with the residents made the population of the town almost double its normal size.

Soon after the dinner hour the crowd all began to move in one direction, for everybody was headed for the exhibition grounds.

Firemen's Field was an ideal place for the celebration. It was in a broad unfenced stretch of valley bottom on the outskirts of town and a

grandstand had been erected there for the Firemen's Tournament in the spring, so well remembered by the "smoke-eaters" of Quarry Troop.
A deep woods stretched along the west side of the
field and Otter Creek formed the southern boun-
dary, while the highway to St. Cloud ran across
its northern extreme. There were several acres
of broad green lawn in front of the grandstand,
and the only obstructions in the whole area were
the tall and short poles the scouts had erected.
These, however, had been placed so as not to in-
terfere with the dancing and other events scheduled for the day.

The grandstand was filled to capacity long before the hour set for the beginning of the ceremonies, and by the time the Mayor and various
other officials had entered their special reviewing
stand hundreds of people were massed in a semi-
circle about the field.

To one side of the entrance was a group of gay
colored tents or marquees, about which were
crowded hundreds of tiny tots, all arrayed in the
gaudy carnival dress. Some were ladies of the
French courts, some were garbed in Colonial cos-

tumes and some were masquerading as bears or as wolves. One group was wearing the wooden shoes and frocks of Holland, another group was costumed as Russian peasants and still others were dressed to represent German, Swedish, Danish and Irish folk. The Campfire Girls were there, too, in a special little marquee by themselves, and to the right of their location was the Quarry Troop, every lad in full uniform, and looking very important.

"Corking crowd, eh, Bruce?" said Nipper Knapp, who stood watching the bank of faces in the grandstand.

"You bet it is. Say, we'll have to do our finest. Not a hitch to-day, fellows," said Bruce.

"Right-o," asserted half a dozen members of the troop enthusiastically.

Then every one became silent, for the director of the carnival had taken the center of the field. A moment he stood there and surveyed his performers, then he gave the signal for the music, and presently the grand march was under way.

Hundreds of youngsters ranging from tiny tots who were to take part in a Mother Goose scene, to the stalwart scouts themselves, formed in line and paraded around the field, passing in front of the stands.

A very impressive scene representing the signing of the Declaration of Independence was the first number on the program. In this, several academy boys took the parts of John Hancock, John Adams and John Dickinson, and the members of the First Congress.

Immediately following came the folk dances, in which scores of pretty girls in costumes executed the national dances of the various foreign countries. These little maids tripped lightly to the fantastic dance music of the people of the old world for fully twenty minutes and as the last group began the final steps of a pretty Scotch fantasy Bruce stood up and mustered the scouts in line.

"We're next, fellows. Now do your finest. Are the tents ready and the rest of the equipment in order? How's ' Old Nanc'?" he called.

But it was needless to ask the question, for the lads had been ready for fully fifteen minutes.

"How about the flag?" asked Bruce, as the little girls danced their way off the field and the band changed to a martial air.

"All safe," said Romper, who had been appointed custodian of the precious bunting.

"Fine!" said the leader of the Owl patrol.

Bugler Benson sounded the call, "Forward, scouts," and the brown-clad column started toward the tall pole near the center of the field, where Mr. Ford, in Scoutmaster's uniform, stood waiting. They marched in scout order with "Old Nanc," laden with the wireless equipment trundling slowly behind them.

For a moment the lads stood in line in front of the grandstand and saluted, then at a word from Mr. Ford they broke ranks, and presently a scout camp was growing before the surprised spectators' eyes. Tents were erected in a jiffy, scouts were scuttling here and there with camp equipment, cooking utensils and firewood. Some were mixing dough, some frying bacon, some cutting wood and some carrying pails of water. Within ten minutes a model scout camp had appeared in the center of Firemen's Field.

But presently the spectators discovered that

they were doing something even more interesting than building camp. A half dozen scouts under the direction of Bruce were unloading queer looking sections of electrical apparatus from the troop's home-made automobile.

While this was being done, Bud Weir strapped on his climbing spurs and began to climb the tall pole, carrying the end of a good strong manila halyard. This he wove through the pulley at the top and soon the scouts were hoisting one end of the wireless aerials up to him. This was quickly adjusted, as was the machinery on the ground, and in a few minutes the wireless station had been assembled and Bruce was at the key, flashing crackling messages into the air.

Applause came from the grandstand, but before the clapping died away, the lads lined up in front of the taller of the two poles again and Romper produced a roll of shining red silk from one of the tents. With this under his arm he took his place before the flagpole and waited, one hand upon the new halyard, which still remained in the pulley. At this sign Mr. Ford stood out and, removing his campaign hat, faced the spectators and the reviewing stand.

"Honored Mayor, ladies and gentlemen," he said, "the boys of Quarry Troop No. 1 have been granted the privilege by the Town Council to present Woodbridge with a city flag. It is our—"

The Assistant Scoutmaster paused here. In the crowd before him he saw scores of frightened faces. He saw men pointing and heard women cry out in terror. He saw children cower and scamper for the protection of the grandstand.

Instantly all turned and looked across the field toward the strip of woods that bordered it, and what they saw paralyzed them with horror.

There on the edge of the wood that bordered the west of the field, shaking his massive head menacingly and pawing the ground, stood Ponto, the great black and white bull of the Lyman stock farm. The most savage animal in Woodbridge had broken through his barrier and, attracted by the applause of the people, had wandered through the woods to Firemen's Field. And the wrath that kindled in his wicked eyes as he stood and

watched the assemblage made even the bravest
scout shudder. For a moment the lads stood as
if robbed of their presence of mind by the unfa-
miliar emergency. But the next instant they were
stirred to action by the rush of some one running
and a cry:

"Quick, scouts, take care of the children. Get
these year kiddies out o' danger. I'll 'tend to
the bull."

This was from a stocky lad with legs slightly
bowed, who pushed through the group of boys
and laid hold of the halyard of the flagpole. In
an instant he had whipped out his jack-knife and
severed the rope. Then he began to haul it out
of the pulley overhead, meanwhile shouting for
the scouts to quiet the already panic-stricken
crowd and hurry the children out of danger.

Bruce gave one look at the boy from Arizona
and in his eyes saw something that told him he
was master of the situation. Then he turned to
the scouts.

"He can handle the bull, boys," he cried;
"come, work fast, get the children back."

And the next instant the scouts, armed with

their staffs, began to herd the tiny tots behind the grandstand, leaving Dick Austin alone in the center of the field.

The lad from Arizona was working frantically. With his knife he cut the flag from the rope and with the line thus freed began to weave a bow-line knot into one end. This he made to serve as the ring for a lariat, and presently he had a fifteen-foot loop spread out before him on the ground. Then with his eyes on the enraged bull he coiled the rest of the rope into his left hand. And all the time he worked his plucky face wore a grim smile.

As for the bull, he stood there grunting and pawing the sod furiously, his fiery eyes fastened on the lone figure.

But it was not in Dick Austin's make-up to flee from a bull. Instead, he shouted:

"Come on, you old son-of-a-gun," and he actually kicked the red silk flag into the air to tantalize the animal. This was too much for the beast. When he saw the red flag flaunted at him by this puny human he let out a bellow and charged.

Dick was on his toes in an instant. With a

twist of his hand he started the loop circling about his head, while his eyes were fastened on the enraged animal charging toward him with lowered head.

Nearer he came! Dick could see the red in his distended nostrils; he could see the cords and arteries in his massive neck and shoulders standing out under his velvety skin. He could feel the ground tremble under the pounding of his heavy feet. The next instant those short, ugly, black-tipped horns might be buried into his flesh and he would be tossed into the air. And if he dropped limp and helpless he would be stamped to death. The beast was twenty feet away now. His head dropped lower for the final plunge. He lunged his great body forward.

But the boy was not there! Like a panther, Dick had leaped behind the flag-pole, but not until he had hurled the whistling loop straight at the charging animal's feet. Then with a quick turn he snubbed the line about the pole.

The next instant the great beast's legs were jerked out from under him and with a roar of rage he turned a complete somersault and crashed to the ground, every bit of his wrath jarred out of him by the stunning impact.

In a twinkle Dick came from behind the pole and with the lariat still in his hands rushed toward the prostrate animal. Two dexterous twists were all he made and the hind legs of the bull were lashed as fast as the front ones and savage Ponto was helpless.

After the members of the Quarry Troop had viewed the municipal fireworks in front of Town Hall that night they gathered at headquarters to discuss the day's events before going home. But there was only one event to be discussed, and that was on the lips of every individual in town.

"By Jove, I called him a coward," said Bud Weir. "But if there's a fellow among us who has as much sand as he had—I—I—well, by cracky, there isn't any."

"Well," said Bruce thoughtfuly. "It's this way—ah—er—I mean— Aw, shucks, I can't express it the way I want to, but he surely didn't shirk the duty for which he was prepared. He told me this morning that lassoing cattle (roping he calls it) and riding horses is part of a day's work where he comes from."

"I don't care if he is skittish about machinery," said Romper Ryan emphatically, "I'm going to see that Dick Austin becomes a scout before he leaves Woodbridge; he's the kind of a chap we need."

CHAPTER XII

BRUCE and two companions, Romper Ryan and Jiminy Gordon, were passing the Post Office just as Morton McCabe, the little old man who delivered mail in the southern district of Woodbridge, came down the broad stone steps.

"How are you, Mr. McCabe?" saluted Bruce.

"Hello, boys; fine, fine, thanks. Say, did you get your letter?" said the diminutive postman, who always talked very fast and tried to crowd as many sentences as he could into a single breath.

"Letter?" demanded Bruce, "what letter?"

"Why, I left a letter up at headquarters for you this morning. It was addressed to you, care of Quarry Troop No. 1, of Woodbridge. Came from Old Harbor Beach, Maine. Saw the postmark. Big letter. Looked important."

"Is that so? Thank you, Mr. McCabe," said Bruce.

"Who do you know at Old Harbor Beach, Bruce?" asked Romper.

"That's what I was wondering. I can't figure it out. The letter must be meant for all of us, or else it wouldn't have been mailed to headquarters. Come on, fellows, we'll see what it is."

Ten minutes later the three lads arrived at headquarters. There was the big blue envelope sticking under the door. Bruce picked it up and ripped it open, while his companions crowded around and looked over his shoulder. Hastily the patrol leader's eyes ran through the first paragraph. Then, as if he could not believe what he had read, he started to go over it again.

"Out loud, out loud. Don't be so blamed stingy," said Romper, who was eager to hear the news it contained.

"I—er—aw, say, this must be a joke. Gee, if it isn't, it's the biggest piece of luck the troop has had in some time. Listen, fellows:

Bruce Clifford, Chief of the Motor Cycle Fire Department,
  Woodbridge, Vt.

MY DEAR BRUCE: From what I have heard of your motorcycle fire department I have come to the conclusion that the members of your troop are exactly the boys I need to help me this summer. I would like to hire the services of ten scouts to take charge of a motorcycle life-saving corps I am organizing at Old Harbor Beach.

I own all the bathing concessions here and we have a strip of the finest beach along the Atlantic Coast. It is fifteen miles long, just as firm as concrete. The bathing here is treacherous at times, however, and there have been several lives lost so far this summer. I do not care to have any more such accidents and I want a good crew of life savers to help me. This crew will cover the beach on especially designed motorcycles. I know you scouts are trained in first aid work and are well fitted for these duties, and that is why I am eager to have your services. Of course I want only the ten best swimmers in the troop.

It is necessary that you come to Old Harbor Beach at once, as the International Automobile Races will be held here next week, and these with several large conventions will bring thousands of people to Old Harbor from now until the end of the summer. I will pay transportation for ten scouts and will board you and pay each of you $5.00 a week. If these terms are satisfactory, wire me at once and I will send a check to cover expenses.

Very truly yours,

J. ARTHUR HERRICK,
President, Old Harbor Improvement Association.

"By Jiminy, what do you think of that?" exclaimed Gordon in amazement.

"Jove, I can't believe it. Seems like a—well, I think some one is making fun of us," said Bruce. "Wait, I'll read it over again and see if I can see a joker in it somewhere." Once more he read it aloud, while Romper and Jiminy Gordon listened.

"Sounds mighty good on second reading," asserted Romper.

"It sure does," exclaimed Gordon enthusiastically, "and just think, fellows, if we go we can see the Internationals. Jove, I was looking over the entry list in the paper this morning. The best automobile drivers in the world will be there—St. Clare, DuBlan, Osterhout, and—and—best of all, Dan Dacy, the American, who has been smashing all of the old records. The papers say Dacy is the favorite. He's going to make a new record in everything from five to fifteen miles and trim the Frenchmen and the Germans an—"

"Oh, say, quit! We're not there yet. Gee, you almost make me believe I'm really going," said Romper.

"But what's to prevent?" demanded Jiminy.

"Well—well—I don't know, unless this letter is a joke."

"We'll find out if it is or not by sending a wire immediately," said Bruce, who had been thinking the situation over.

"Yes, but first why not get the troop together and see if we can get ten good swimmers whose parents will let them go? We can call a meeting this afternoon and send our telegram to-night," said Romper.

"Right-o; good suggestion," said Jiminy.

"And I really think we should submit the whole thing to Mr. Ford and get his opinion before we take definite action. If some one is joshing us, he'll be able to see through it all right."

But subsequent events proved conclusively that the letter was not a joke. The scouts called their meeting immediately, and after a careful study of the troop's merit badge list, and a painful process of elimination, the ten oldest and best fitted scouts of the troop were selected to become members of the life-saving crew. Then Bruce, Romper and Jiminy took the letter to Mr. Ford and gave him the whole details of the case.

Mr. Ford read the letter slowly, carefully considering every detail. Then he laid it down and removed his glasses.

"Well, boys, if you want my opinion on the whole matter, I would say that you were quite the luckiest lot of chaps I've ever heard of. I spent a summer in Old Harbor Beach three years ago, and, of course, I met Mr. Herrick. He is quite the finest man I ever hope to come in contact with; big, stout and jovial, and as good-hearted as can be. If your parents will let you, I would advise every one to accept the offer.''

"Cracky, we *are* in luck, fellows. I move we telegraph our acceptance right away,'' said Romper.

"I move we turn the matter over to Mr. Ford and let him telegraph. He's our Scoutmaster, and I'm sure Mr. Herrick would feel better about the whole thing if he found he was dealing with a grown-up person,'' said Bruce.

"Right,'' said Jiminy and Romper.

"Well, if that's how the wind lies, I'll do it,'' said Mr. Ford; "only you boys consult your parents first and tell me what they have to say.''

"Whoop-e-e, we will see the Internationals!'' exclaimed Jiminy.

"Yes, and we get a month at the seashore. When'll we start?'' demanded Romper.

"Just as soon as the money arrives. About

Tuesday, I should guess," said Bruce, as the lads left Mr. Ford's house.

It is hardly natural for ten thoroughly healthy scouts to be confined to the restricted limits of a day coach for four solid hours without becoming extremely weary of the monotony of it all. Bruce and the rest of the members of Quarry Troop No. 1 became quite restive before the long journey to Old Harbor Beach ended.   Indeed, the lads were thoroughly pleased when, after the engine whistle had emitted a prolonged shriek, the conductor poked his head in at the door and drawled—"Old Har-b-o-r—, Old Harbor Beach! Next stop Port Junction."

"Thank goodness we're here at last," exclaimed Nipper Knapp, as he began to gather his luggage together.

"That's the best news I've heard to-day," insisted Bud Weir, swinging his suitcase to his shoulder and crowding out into the aisle with the rest of the scouts.

A stout good-natured looking man with a little five-year-old girl in a bathing suit perched on his

shoulder and a big collie dog romping by his side,
was easily the most conspicuous individual on the
long station platform. Bruce caught sight of him
as he descended the steps of the coach.

"That's Mr. Herrick, or I'm a duffer at guess-
ing," he said to Romper, who was just behind him.

"You're not a duffer, for here he comes to welcome us," said Ray Martin, who had overheard
the remark.

Indeed, as soon as the big man saw the group
of uniformed scouts leaving the train he hurried
toward them.

"Hello, there, boys. I'm the one you're looking
for, I guess. My name's Herrick."

"My name is Bruce Clifford, Mr. Herrick," said
the patrol leader, extending his hand, "and these
are the life-savers you have been looking for."

"Good, I'll learn your names later, boys, and if
I don't, I'll give you names that'll be just as
good, won't I, May? Boys, this is my daughter
May. Now come along with me to my office on
the pier and I'll outline just what my plans are.
I want you to go on guard as soon as you can, for
the crowd at the beach is getting larger with

every train that pulls in. The Internationals start to-morrow, you know. The racing cars are all here. For a week past they have been tearing up and down the beach from sunrise until the bathers begin to turn out for their morning dip. Sort of tuning up for the big events."

"Will we be able to see the races?" asked Gordon eagerly.

"I don't see why not. They start to-morrow and will last for three days," replied Mr. Herrick.

"Won't that be great," exclaimed several as they fell in line behind Mr. Herrick and accompanied him through the resort toward the pier.

Old Harbor Beach was like all other high-class watering places along the Atlantic Coast, only a great deal larger than the average. At least a dozen tremendous hotels were located on the heights back of the beach. There were the usual number of shore restaurants and candy stores, too, and a board walk that stretched along the entire waterfront. Below this was a great wide beach of pure white sand as firm as a well-paved road, and fairly crowded with bathers. This beach was known throughout the world as an automobile race course, and many a speed record had been made on it.

"So this is the famous Old Harbor Beach race course?" said Jiminy, as he eyed the straight-away.

"That's what it is, son, and if you'll look away down there you'll see a number of low green sheds. Those are the garages where the speed maniacs store their high-powered cars."

"Jiminy!" whispered Gordon, thoroughly awed.

Mr. Herrick's office was in the big white building at the shore end of the steel recreation pier. Without any ceremony he ushered the lads into the room and had them make themselves at home. This invitation the scouts accepted by promptly taking a seat on whatever was handiest, including window sills, tables and even the floor; Mr. Herrick sat down at his desk, while the collie curled up at his feet and his daughter took her place on his knee.

"Scouts," he said, "there have been three very sad occurrences at the beach this Summer, and while in each case the fault lay entirely with the bather, I feel very much disturbed by the accidents, and I don't want any more to take place this year. I have called upon you boys to help me prevent them. Remember, from now on you lads are the guardians of the lives of bathers at Old Harbor Beach.'' He spoke the last sentence very impressively.

"Here's my plan," he continued after a pause. "Last Winter I was out to California, and at one of the beaches I saw a motorcycle life-saving corps that had been organized by an old-time life-saver. It pleased me so much that I decided to have the same sort of a patrol on my beach. I ordered two motorcycles built along the lines of the machines used there. They arrived here two days ago and are now in their garages waiting for you. These cars are equipped with all kinds of life-saving and first-aid devices, including a stretcher, a pulmotor, bandages and medicines of all kinds. There will be two men to a motorcycle; a driver and a man on the tandem seat, ready to spring from the wheel and plunge into the surf and make a rescue. He should be the best swimmer of the pair, of course.

"All along the beach I have had signal towers built, each of which will be manned by a scout. He will keep constant vigil, and, at the first sign of trouble in his vicinity, he will flash a warning to the next tower. The scouts in that tower will flash the signal on until it reaches the lookout at the garage. Then the motorcycle will be off to the scene of trouble, tearing down the beach at a mile-a-minute clip. How does that strike you?"

"Great," exclaimed several of the scouts in unison.

"Well, don't get the idea that it's all fun. Indeed, it's mighty serious business, I'll have you know. On your quickness to respond to an alarm and upon your bravery and cool-headedness in a crisis will depend a human life, perhaps several of them," said Mr. Herrick.

"We realize that," said Bruce soberly.

"I guess you'll do, all right. I've heard a great deal about you Vermont scouts and I guess you'll be able to do what I ask of you and do it right. Now, if you are ready, we'll go down to one of the garages; there are two of them. If you will look out of the window you will see one about a mile down the beach there.   The other is a mile to the north of us.   The distance between the two stations includes all of the beach reserved for bathers and it will give each machine about a mile to patrol.

"The garages have just been completed.   Each will contain sleeping accommodations for five boys.   You will divide your crew into two patrols, with a leader for each patrol.   One patrol will occupy the north station and the other the south. There will be two life savers and three watchmen to each patrol.   Do you understand?"

"Indeed, we do," said Bruce.

"Good," said Mr. Herrick.   Then, after sending his little daughter out on to the beach to romp with her collie companion, he continued: "Come on and we'll inspect your new quarters."   And, with Mr. Herrick in the lead the scouts filed out upon the pier and down a long iron stairway to the beach below.

Through crowds of bathers the lads made their way until they arrived at a long, low structure built near the board walk.   This was the south station.

Carpenters and painters were putting the finishing touches on to the building, and it looked to the scouts as if they were going to have a capital home in which to spend the month of August.

Inside the big double doors were two rooms. The rear room was equipped with five white iron beds and several chiffoniers and wash stand, while the front apartment contained the life guard's motorcycle.

"Jiminy, look at that machine," exclaimed Gordon, who was the first one to enter the building.

"Cracky, it's the best make on the market, too," said Nipper Knapp, examining the maker's name plate.

"Bet it will burn up the beach, eh, fellows?" said Romper.

"It sure will. It's a two-cylinder tandem. It'll make fifty miles an hour, or I'm no judge," said Bruce enthusiastically.

"Like it, boys?" queried Mr. Herrick, who had been watching them as they inspected the apparatus.

"Like it! Gee, we couldn't help but like it. It's a corker. But what's that side car paraphernalia, that long box and the cigar-shaped tin can and the reel with wire cable on it, and all that?"

"I'll explain that to you right away," said Mr. Herrick. "That long, flat-topped box on the side car serves several purposes. When you want to take an unconscious person to the emergency hospital over on Beach Avenue you can use the box as a stretcher. Just put your patient on to the top of it and while the man on the tandem seat holds him fast the driver can rush the machine off to its destination at top speed; regular mile-a-minute ambulance service, you see.

"Under that flat top are a lot of interesting things. The box contains several compartments in which are all sorts of first-aid preparations, including bandages, medicines, aromatic stimulants and the like. And, last of all, there is a pulmotor."

"Oh, I've heard of the pulmotor and always wanted to see one in use," said Bud.

"Well, I'll tell you how they work," said Mr. Herrick. "It is the latest thing in the way of first-aid appliances. It pumps oxygen into the lungs of an unconscious person automatically.

Firemen and life savers all over the world are using them now. That blue tank there contains oxygen. This machinery under the glass covering is a pump that works by the pressure of the oxygen. A little of the oxygen escapes from the tank and moves the pump, which forces the life-giving gas into those long pipes. That muzzle at the end of the pipes is placed over the victim's mouth and nose, and in that way the oxygen enters the lungs. You boys can study the directions for its use on the cover of the box here. When you have a pulmotor around you won't have to resort to the artificial respiration drill described in your Handbook. Try it out on each other until you know exactly how to handle it.''

''You bet we will. We'll work out a regular rescue exercise, won't we, fellows?'' said Bruce.

''Right-o!'' exclaimed half a dozen lads in unison.

''Fine. Now, I'll explain the way a rescue is made by the California life savers. That reel of wire cable and the cigar-shaped float attached to the rear end of the side car is a very important factor in rescue work. The float has a life belt attached to it, as you can see. When a rescue is to be made the motorcycle comes to a stop at the water's edge and the man on the tandem seat leaps off and seizes the float. He buckles the life belt on to him as he plunges into the water and the man on shore reels out the cable as the rescuer swims to the person in trouble. When the life saver reaches the man or woman he is after he does not have to struggle to keep afloat, for the buoy holds him on top of the water. If he has to dive for the drowning one, he merely unbuckles the life belt and when he comes to the surface the buoy is right there for him to seize hold of, or, if he chose to, he could strap it fast to the one he is trying to save. The wire cable is very light, but very strong, and when the buoy is made fast to any one, the man on shore hauls away and drags the body out, just as he would haul out a big fish.''

"Jove, but *that's* an outfit for you," exclaimed Romper.

"Well, I'm glad you like it, Scouts. The outfit in the north station is identically the same. I didn't spare any money to have your equipment the finest.''

"That's mighty good of you," said Bruce.

"Why, it's to my own interest, lads. A single life saved is worth more to me than all the money I've put into this scheme. Now it's up to you boys to make good my investment."

"We'll do it," shouted the scouts in unison.

"Alright, boys, that's all I ask. I'll leave you now. You can organize your own patrols and select your own leaders without my help. When you get hungry, go to the Pine Grove Hotel. I've arranged to have all your meals served to you there.

"You can spend the rest of the afternoon becoming familiar with the apparatus, and I guess you'll have all the time you want to practice during the next two or three days, for while the races are on no bathers will be allowed on the beach. Well, good-by and good luck to you."

And the genial bath house proprietor left the scouts to their own devices.

"Jiminy, fellows, I can't believe it. Some one pinch me, please. I want to see if I'm awake. Just think of being in charge of such an outfit," said Gordon after Mr. Herrick had left.

"It does seem like a dream, doesn't it?" said Bruce, examining the contents of the first-aid chest that formed the body of the side car. "Come on, let's dig into this and see what we have to work with."

That invitation was unnecessary, for several of the lads were rummaging through the chest while others were inspecting the machine and still others were wandering through the building looking their new quarters over. So occupied were they in this pleasant occupation that they completely forgot the time. Indeed, it was after six o'clock before they realized it. And since six o'clock was the dinner hour at the hotel the lads hustled off up the beach to find their boarding place.

For an hour after they left the hotel the scouts wandered through the resort acquainting themselves with the place. At eight they all returned to the south station, for they realized that they still had a great deal to do that evening.

When the electric lights were lit and the scouts were comfortably situated in the bedroom of the station, Bruce called a meeting. The four best swimmers were selected first. They were Jiminy,

Romper, Bud and Bruce. After a vote Jiminy and Bruce were selected to man the motorcycle in the south station, while the two others were appointed operators of the apparatus in the north station. The six remaining lads were appointed lookouts to man the beach towers. Three were attached to the north station crew, of which Bud was made leader, and the other three were appointed members of Bruce's south station crew.

Before the meeting adjourned it was decided that all ten scouts remain in the south station for the night, since there would be very little work for them to do next day. Bruce also thought it wise to have all the lads together while they were learning to use the pulmotor and becoming familiar with their apparatus. Then, too, the south station was better located to afford the lads a view of the automobile races next morning, which counted for a great deal.

By sleeping two in a bed and disregarding any slight discomforts the ten lads found that they could occupy quarters meant to accommodate only five. And after a round of pillow fights and similar nocturnal diversions they were finally all tucked in and ready for sleep.

"Well, good-night, fellows. Hope we all sleep comfortably," shouted Romper after the lights had been turned out.

"Good-night yourself," shouted Jiminy. Then he added, "Hi, fellows, the Internationals to-morrow! Whoop—e-e-e!"

CHAPTER XIII

THE DAY OF THE BIG RACE

BANG—bang-bankety-bang-bang-bang! The ten scouts bounded out of bed at once. All were wide eyed with excitement and wonder.

"What the dickens! An earthquake!" demanded Bud Weir.

Jiminy Gordon was the first one to the window.

"Gee whiz, look at him go!"

"Look at who—what?"

"Why that was one of the racing cars," said Jiminy. "They are tuning up for the big races to-day. Guess it was a foreign car from the racket it made. All the mufflers off. Couldn't make out just which car it was though. Going so fast it looked just like a gray streak. I—"

"Bur-r-r-r-r bumpety-boom-boom-boom-b a n g-bang-bang!"

"Whoopee-e-e, here's another one," screamed Jiminy.

The ten scouts rushed to the front door of the building, ignoring the fact that they were clad only in pajamas and night shirts, and waved to the passing racer.

"Cracky, look at him tear up the beach," exclaimed Bruce.

"Rather early in the morning to risk one's neck, eh? It's only four o'clock. Guess they are doing their last tuning up before the events start," said Jiminy.

"Say, how do they race?" asked fat Babe Wilson. "Do they line 'em up like a lot of sprinters and start 'em when a pistol is fired?"

"Well, they may do some match racing to-morrow, but to-day I think they will hold their time trials. They will race to see who can make the best time over the course," said Jiminy.

"How fast can they go?" asked Ray Martin.

"Oh, they can make a mile in half a minute. The world's record for a mile is twenty-five and one-half seconds," said Gordon, who was more or less of an authority on automobiles among the members of the Quarry Troop.

"Gee Whizz! Say what can they make fifteen

miles in? How long will it take 'em to go the full length of the beach?" asked Bruce.

"Well, the world's record for fifteen miles is just ten minutes flat. That's an old record and Dan Dacy says he's going to smash it to smithereens to-day. Hope he does. Say, fellows, what do you say to going down and looking over the garages before breakfast?"

"Fine, let's get some clothes on and we'll start right away," said Romper.

Dressing was only a matter of a few minutes and presently the troop was on its way down the boardwalk toward the point where the series of green-peaked roofs located the garages of the speed maniacs. Although it was not yet five o'clock in the morning there were scores of people on the board walk all headed in the same direction.

"Say, this is going to be a big day all right," said Ray Martin, as he noted the enthusiasm that prevailed.

"Right-o, just look at the crowd down there at the garages already this morning," said Bruce.

About each of the low houses were grouped

dozens of curiosity seekers. The scouts soon joined the throng and began to inspect the quarters of the races. Each garage contained a big sullen looking car about which was grouped half a dozen mechanics. These men were tinkering here, tightening a bolt there, or wiping and polishing the great machines as if they were so many sacred elephants. Mechanical parts, pumps, jacks, boxes of tools, cans of oil, extra tires and wheels, cushions and innumerable odds and ends were scattered about each building and everybody seemed to be keyed up to an extreme nervous pitch. On every side could be heard remarks about the cars and drivers, their records and their chances for winning the various events.

The excitement was infectious and before they realized it the scouts were as thoroughly interested as every one else. They began to talk automobiles to all with whom they came in contact and soon picked up a great deal of information about the notables who were to take part in the races.

"Say, Bruce," said Jiminy Gordon suddenly, "there's Dan Dacy. See him. That big, tall, light-haired fellow down there. I've seen his picture so many times that I almost feel as if I know him. Come on, we'll go down and see his machine. That must be his garage—yes, it is. See the sign over the door. Vix-Benson, it says. That's the car he's going to drive.''

The scouts followed Jiminy and Bruce and soon found themselves part of a very large crowd gathered about the famous driver's headquarters. Dacy was the favorite American in the race and since he was to operate one of the best known American cars everybody was enthusiastic to see him carry off the honors of the event in which he was entered. He was standing by the door of his garage watching his attendants tinker with his machine, when the scouts came up. The lads pushed their way through the crowd to reach the rope railing about the entrance to the garage, and when the tall racer saw them, he smiled and waved his hand.

''How are you, Scouts?'' he said good-naturedly. Then without waiting for an answer he came over to the rope.

''Where are you fellows from?'' he demanded.

''Woodbridge, Vermont, sir,'' said Bruce.

"Woodbridge, Vermont? Well, you came a long way to see the races, didn't you?" he said, a boyish smile playing about the corners of his mouth.

"Well, not exactly. You see we are here on business. That is, we've been hired as life guards at Old Harbor. We're going to patrol the beach for the rest of the Summer.

"Oh-ho, so you are the chaps Mr. Herrick was telling me about—have motorcycles and all that sort of rigging, eh? Say, boys, that's a great scheme. I saw the original motor cycle life guards work out in California last year, and they're great, too. Hope you have luck." Then after shaking hands with Bruce and Jiminy and two or three other scouts, he turned and entered the garage, for one of his mechanics had called him.

And although Dan Dacy did not realize it, this spirit of democracy had won him ten thoroughly capable rooters, for the scouts were more than pleased with his friendship.

"Say isn't he a corking fine chap," exclaimed Bruce.

"I should say he was; a regular pippin' I'd

call him," said Jiminy stoutly. And he looked at his companions as if he dared any one of them to deny it.

The crowd about the garage was growing to tremendous proportions, and it was all that the scouts could do to extricate themselves. When they finally reached the open beach again, Bruce looked at his watch.

"Say, fellows, it's getting late," he exclaimed; "it's six o'clock and we haven't had any breakfast. I think we will have to hustle over to the hotel if we want to get back to quarters and have a drill before the races start."

"Right-o," exclaimed Babe Wilson, "I know it's getting late because my stomach feels all shriveled up for want of something to eat."

"Huh, that stomach of yours," said Jiminy Gordon in disgust, as he took a lingering look toward the garages. A moment later he fell in line with the rest of the lads, who started up the board walk toward the hotel.

On their way back the scouts paid a brief visit to the north station, but they all returned to Bruce's domain at half-past seven, for the north station crew was rather eager to stay in the vicinity of the lower station for a better view of the races. Then, too, they had decided the night before that it would be well for all of them to practice their first aid work together.

There was very little need for the lookouts to man their tower during this practice work, for they needed no drilling since all of their signaling would be done with signal flags and the semaphore signal code which is part of the examination for all second class scouts.

That being the case, Bruce decided that all of the lads would devote the morning to operating the pulmotor, while the four life savers made frequent plunges into the surf so as to become accustomed to swimming with the aid of the buoy. One after another the lads operated the pulmotor upon a supposed victim until each had learned the proper method of adjusting and strapping fast the mouthpiece, and which screws to turn to start and stop the oxygen pump. An hour of this practice work was quite sufficient, and when it was finished Bruce and Jiminy and Bud and Romper, turn about, took the motor cycle for short dashes up the beach and indulged in a mock rescue. At ten o'clock the drilling was stopped, for the racing automobiles began to appear on the beach in final preparation for the races which were scheduled to start at eleven.

"Say, fellows, that rescue work is some fun," said Jiminy Gordon, as he emerged from the surf for the last time and came toward the station.

"You bet it is," said Bruce, as he shut off the power of the motorcycle and wheeled the machine into its quarters.

"And the water is just snappy enough to feel good, too. You know, I think I'll stay in my bathing suit all day, even though there won't be any bathers to rescue. I want to get tanned up right away," added Jiminy.

"Good idea," exclaimed several, with enthusiasm, and forthwith they all donned the special maroon bathing suits that Mr. Herrick had provided for his life guards. But it is hard to tell whether it was the desire to acquire a good coat of tan or the opportunity afforded them to display their rather pretentious bathing suits, that moved them to take this step. However, fifteen minutes later, a group of ten uniformed and more or less self-conscious beach guards were sunning themselves in front of the south station in full view of the thousands of people who were gathering on the board walk to view the races.

By eleven o'clock the crowd had increased to a veritable horde. Thousands lined the board walk from the garages to the finish line and hundreds of automobiles were parked in every roadway. Special guards, composed of the local troop of boy scouts with their staffs and a troop of militia from Portland had been detailed to keep the sightseers orderly and in position on the board walk. They were all having their hands full accomplishing the task, however, for the automobile enthusiasts began to get restless as the time for the start of the races drew near.

At five minutes after eleven the band on the recreation pier, which had been blaring forth popular airs for an hour, ceased, and a moment later the judges made their appearance on the beach. This was a signal for prolonged cheering on the part of the crowd. But the noise stopped when a single individual carrying a black and

white flag stepped out into the course and began
wigwagging. He was signaling to another indi،
vidual at the garages, who in turn transmitted his
signal to the starting line in the dim distance
down the beach.

"That means everything is ready. The first
car will start in a moment," said Jiminy Gordon
nervously.

Every one was gazing down the beach, where a
tiny black blotch on the sand marked the dozen or
more racing cars held ready for the start. Then
when every one was waiting tense and silent—
Boom! came the muffled echo of the starting gun
—They're off! cried the crowd, and far, far down
the beach the scouts could see the tiniest black
speck coming toward them. Soon they heard a
curious far-off drone which developed quickly
into a grumble, then into a fusillade of loud bangs
as the racing car approached. The scouts were
all on their feet now, nervous and expectant.

"Osterhout, the German," cried the spectators,
as the long, low racer drew near.

Then almost before the scouts could wink, it
had roared past, its hood enveloped in blue flames

and its driver bending low over the steering gear.

"Gee whiz!" was all that the amazed scouts could say when the big car roared across the line.

A brief but tense silence followed the finish of the run, for the crowd waited while the judges, by means of an elaborate system of telephone communicated with the starters, fixed the time. Presently, however, the huge scoreboard on the recreation pier displayed: Osterhout, two minutes 34 seconds. This announcement was greeted by a roar, for the German had equaled the world record for five miles.

"Cracky," cried Jiminy Gordon, "Dan Dacy will have to go some to beat that. Just think, if Osterhout had been one-fifth of a second faster he'd have smashed the world's record. Gosh, I wish—"

Boom! Here comes another one!

Silence reigned in the vast crowd again and every eye followed the black speck. "Du Blon," guessed some; "St. Clare," said others; "Wolverton," asserted several enthusiasts.

But before the big racer had traveled half of

the course the hum of its engines ceased and the black speck gradually came to a halt. Wolverton it proved to be and his car had developed engine trouble. The Stafford car was out of the race.

St. Clare and Du Blon followed in quick succession, each of them driving their madly flying vehicles to the limit of endurance, but each fell behind Osterhout's mark by several seconds. McCalkin, the ruddy-faced Irish driver, was the next sensation. His was the smallest car of the race in point of length. Indeed, it looked as if it had collided with a telegraph pole and lost most of its hood. But under that snub nose were concealed six perfectly good cylinders that spat fire all the way down the course and shot the car over the finish line two seconds better than the world's record. What a roar of applause greeted the boyish driver when the figures were displayed! Even the scouts forgot for a moment that they were rooting exclusively for Dan Dacy and burst forth in a ringing cheer.

But presently their attention was diverted from this achievement, for word was passed from the judges' stand that Dan Dacy with his Vix-Benson was the next contestant.

"Dan Dacy next!" was the word that passed from mouth to mouth through the crowd. Every one was a-tip-toe with excitement. All eyes were strained on the starting line.

"Gee, I hope he comes through with a new record," said Bruce anxiously.

"He will," asserted Jiminy Gordon positively.

Boom! Five thousand pairs of eyes were fastened on the tiny black speck that detached itself from the black blot far down the beach, and sped northward. Ten thousand ears were strained to catch the first far-off hum of the motor.

Dacy was coming. His Vix-Benson was burning up the beach. Now the scouts caught the buzz of the motor. It grew louder with the passing of every second. Like a black projectile the car came on, flames from the throbbing cylinders licking about the hood.

"Dacy! Dacy! Danny Dacy! Make it a new record!" screamed the electrified crowd while he was yet two miles from the finish line. Unquestionably he was the favorite.

On came the roaring racer. The car was just a gray blur that hardly seemed to touch the beach, and begoggled Dan Dacy looked like the hooded messenger of death.

Then with an ear-splitting roar the great machine passed the scouts on the last mile of the course!

"By Jiminy, it's a new record or I'll— Oh, mercy! Look! Look! She'll be killed!"

The scouts stood transfixed with horror. Up the beach in the very path of the flying motor stood little May Herrick, clutching a red rubber ball in her hand and looking at the coming machine with horror written in every line of her childish face.

The whole situation was clear. The tot had dropped her ball, which had rolled out onto the sloping beach. With her mind only on rescuing the plaything, she had pulled herself out of her nurse's grasp and run out onto the race course. And then when she found herself in the path of certain death she had become panic-stricken.

Dan Dacy's heart must have leapt to his throat when he saw the little one in his way. But if it

did it in no way affected his nerve.   He knew that
to turn the steering wheel but an inch meant certain destruction to the careening car and a broken
neck for himself perhaps.   Yet he braved this
hideous fate and wrenched at the steering gear.

There was a terrific roar, a crash of shattered
metal and in a cloud of sand the big gray racer
turned abruptly and plunged end over end down
the beach into the curling breakers.   The crowd
gave vent to a shriek of alarm when they saw Dan
Dacy's limp form shoot clear of the wreck and go
whirling, arms and legs flying out toward the
point where the combers were breaking.

Like every one of the five thousand witnesses
of the tragedy, the scouts stood paralyzed for a
moment—but only for a moment—Bruce was the
first to gather his scattered wits.

"Quick, Jiminy!   We'll get him!   Come!   He
may still be alive!   The rest of you fellows follow
on foot!"

While he was speaking, Bruce rushed into the
station and started the motor cycle.   Jiminy was
right behind him and an instant later the powerful machine was making forty miles an hour over

the sandy beach.   Bruce bent low over the handle bars while Jiminy clung on and sought to buckle the life buoy belt about his waist.

When the machine reached the wrecked motor car Bruce brought it to an abrupt stop.   But already Jiminy had leaped from the machine and plunged into the water.   With powerful over-hand strokes he breasted the breakers.   He seemed to shoot through the water, so mighty were his efforts.

Thirty feet out he saw something bobbing upon the surface of the water.   It was Dacy's leather helmet.   Toward this Jiminy headed and the water fairly boiled with the struggle he was making to reach the spot.   In a few seconds he was near enough to reach out and grasp the black object.   But he let go of it immediately and the next moment he was seen to prepare for a dive under the surface.   A few feet away he had seen some air bubbles coming to the top.

In a jiffy he had unbuckled the life buoy.   Then like a seal the lithe youngster sought the dark green depths, following the line of bubbles.   Down he swam, deeper and deeper, for on the white,

sandy bottom he could see a dark, shapeless mass
turning round and round with the action of the
water. He reached out to seize it and his fingers
slipped from the driver's leather jacket. Again
he tried, and his hand closed about the cold wrist
of the unconscious man.

Then he turned and started to struggle upward,
dragging his heavy burden after him. It was
hard work—terrible work, for he had dived deep
and he was badly in need of air. His lungs felt
as if they would burst. The blood pressure in his
neck and head was almost unbearable. At first
he could make no headway. The drowning man
seemed to hold fast to the bottom. But he fought
hard for he realized that if he let go of Dacy he
would have difficulty in finding him with a second
dive. Every moment was precious, too. There
might still be a spark of life in the limp form he
was trying to rescue.

Up, up, he struggled. Above he could see the
light of day. Great green bubbles raced past him.
Only a few feet now. Only a second or two longer. Thus did he spur himself onward until suddenly his head shot clear of the waves, and, with

a gasp, he filled his tortured lungs with new air.

Ten feet away danced the cigar-shaped float with its life belt, and swimming toward him from the crowded beach were two other scouts ready to help.

Jiminy summoned every ounce of his remaining stength and held the head of the unconscious man above the water. And when the spectators saw that he had actually made the rescue a cheer louder and longer than any that had greeted the racers rent the air.

It was hard work and Jiminy was at the point of exhaustion, yet he tried his utmost to buckle the life belt about poor Dacy. But while he fumbled with the straps the two other scouts arrived and relieved him of the task. Quickly the belt was adjusted and the sign flashed to Bruce, who seized the steel cable and hauled away.

Then the two lads turned their attention to Jiminy and between them aided him into shallow water.

By the time the three swimmers reached the beach the scouts had cleared Dacy's lungs of water and had started the pulmotor. For twenty minutes the lads worked valiantly, doing everything that they could to bring back life in the unconscious man, while the anxious crowd looked on.

Finally their efforts were rewarded. Dacy's eyelids quivered several times, then slowly opened, whereat the crowd gave a mad cry of joy and the scouts had all they could do to keep them from pressing closer.

But one man did break through the circle of guards and the lads let him pass. He was Mr. Herrick. Tears of joy coursed down his good-natured face when he saw that Dacy was still alive, and before the scouts could restrain him he seized the prostrate man's hand and squeezed it while he murmured:

"Dacy, Dacy, thank goodness you are still alive. I was afraid you had sacrificed your life to save that little girl of mine."

Then turning toward Bruce, he said, "Scouts, I don't know how to thank you for this. I—"

"Don't try to thank us, Mr. Herrick," said Bruce, "but you can help us put him onto the side car. I think we should get to a doctor's right away, for there may be some broken bones or internal injuries."

And a few moments later the life guard's motorcycle was carrying its first patient to the emergency hospital.

CHAPTER XIV

WHEN THE UNEXPECTED HAPPENED

WHACK — "Nine - hundred - en - ten;" whack — "nine-hundred-en-'leven," whack, "Zare ees almoost une tousan trees what you boys mus' cut awraty. What you zink of zat?" said Paul Nez, the big French-Canadian lumber cruiser, as he hacked a blaze into a six-inch poplar and left his short hatchet wedged fast while he felt through his pockets for a handkerchief.

"Et will take you all ze Wintair for ze work mebbe, huh?" he continued, as he blew his nose with a loud blast.

"George! I shouldn't wonder if it would take us a couple of months at least," said Bruce Clifford as he sat down upon a stump and pushed his hat back upon his head.

"Yes, snow will be thick through here when we finally finish, I guess," added Jiminy Gordon, surveying the forest.

"Well, the Doctair Lyman he say he not in such great rush," smiled the Canadian. Then he paused and seemed to search into the very heart of the wood with his coal black eyes, and all this time he kept sniffing the air.

"Camp 'round here sure. One no good camp too, mebby," said he finally as he pointed toward the west.

"I thought I smelled the smoke of a camp fire," said Bruce.

"So did I," added Jiminy.

"I smell heem smoke, I smell heem scraps, too. No good camp, no know woods. Mebby heem get seek. Come on. We all through now. We find 'em wood road now soon. Doctair Lyman heem line run cross by that blaze over tair; you see heem, huh? Heem end of Doctair Lyman's wood."

"So that's the line, eh? Well, twenty-five acres of woods is a lot of territory, isn't it, Bruce?" said Jiminy, as he picked up his scout hatchet and slipped into his belt.

The Canadian wrenched his hatchet free from the poplar and started swinging westward between the trees and the two Quarry Troop scouts fell in behind him in single file. And as they walked on the smell of the camp fire, and the tainted odor that emanates from a camp's garbage dump grew stronger to their nostrils.

Then presently the camp itself loomed up at the very side of the wood road for which the Canadian lumberman was headed.

A single wall tent of large proportions was the most conspicuous thing about the place. This had its flaps pinned back and in the doorway, reclining on a collapsible canvas camp chair with a bandage-swathed foot propped up on a soap box sat one of the occupants.

The woodsman and the two Quarry Scouts needed only a glance at the little clearing to know that those who had built it here knew nothing at all about the woods and were, moreover, very disorderly by nature. Blankets lay in a confused heap among leaves and twigs instead of being hung up to dry; empty cans, paste board boxes and scraps of paper littered the place; fire burned entirely too near a dry brush pile and there was no stone fireplace to hold it in check; loose papers were scattered about and to make matters even worse, the pots and pans that had been used to cook the last meal lay on the ground unwashed.

It was indeed a bungle of a camp but if the single occupant realized it he did not seem to care a whit for he sat serenely in the doorway of the tent so interested in a book that he did not hear Paul Nez and his young companions approaching.

" 'Allo, you get heem broke foot, mebby?" said Paul with a grin as he moved toward the tent.

The camper looked up with a start, and then smiled. "Yes, I twisted my right ankle yesterday by falling down a gully, and ouch—don't make me move 'cause it hurts like sin. Glad it isn't sprained though. It ought to be well in four or five days. Anything you want? Anything we can do for you? If there is, go ahead and do it yourself. The rest of the fellows are off partridge hunting. What do you want, provisions, matches? I'll tell you where they are and you can help yourself. I can't move."

"We don't want heem nothin'. We go out of woods now right off, down wood road. Why you

don't fix heem camp up good? Look um fire—
poor, bad, very worse. Some day heem catch
bush so, leaves mebby, and then heem timber fire.
Burn out heem woods. Look um pans, pots, dirty
dishes. Not good for smell. Not good for men in
heem woods. Blankets, look um all get lousy.
Not very good camp, heem," said the Canadian,
plainly showing his disgust at the general disorder
about the place.

"I know it, old chap. It looks like the sloppiest
kind of a place to me, but then I'm not supposed
to know anything about camps and woods. I
come from Boston, you see. The other fellows
are the campers. They are Vermonters, from St.
Cloud City," said the man in the doorway sarcastically.

"Huh, a deuced of a lot they know about the
woods and camping," said Bruce in disgust as he
surveyed the scene.

"They know more about keeping a pig sty,"
said Jiminy Gordon as he picked up the blankets
and, shaking them free of the dust, hung them
onto the branch of a nearby hemlock.

"Thanks, old chap, those blankets on the ground

worried me a lot. And if you don't mind, will you scrape up a few of those papers? Jack and Bart (they are the fellows who are camping with me) run off every morning and leave a mess like that behind. They are off hunting most of the day and here I have to sit like a blooming invalid until they come back. But I don't mind so long as I have a good book. Thanks, that looks much better, doesn't it? I'm much obliged to you fellows—ah—er, what're your names anyway—mine's Dave— Dave Connors.''

The two scouts introduced themselves and then because Paul Nez had started down the wood road they waved farewell to the camper with the injured foot and hustled to catch up to the timber cruiser.

"When you come into heem woods for cut um down?" asked the Canadian when the scouts finally caught up with him.

"Why we are going to start cutting right away," said Bruce. "You see we get a fall vacation and that will help a lot. School closes tomorrow and remains closed until next Monday. The whole troop is coming up to Long Lake to-morrow afternoon after school closes, to start a camp and remain here the whole week. Then after that we are going to come up every Friday night and work all day Saturday until our contract is completed and we have enough lumber to build our log camp." They swung along down the wood toward Long Lake where they met the main highway that led back toward Woodbridge and Scout Headquarters.

The members of the Quarry Troop of Woodbridge had taken upon themselves a real contract. Indeed they felt that they had suddenly all become genuine business men as a result of a bargain they had made with the leading physician of the village, for you see their little stroke of dickering had put them in the way of securing material for a real log cabin on the shores of Long Lake, a site for the cabin, and a chance to make a little money for the troop treasury besides. It had come about this way.

Mr. Ford, the Assistant Scoutmaster of the Quarry Troop, had learned from Dr. Lyman that he intended to cut a great deal of the standing timber on his tract of twenty-five acres bordering

the lake. This he intended to dispose of as pulp
wood, the only purpose it was really good for.
Mr. Ford had imparted this information to Bruce
Clifford and Jiminy Gordon that same evening
and it was not long before the leader of the Owl
Patrol and his chum had discovered the possibili-
ties of a business deal.

Accordingly after the next meeting the two lads
visited Dr. Lyman and made him a proposition to
the effect that the scouts would cut his pulp wood
and take their pay in trees. These trees, the lads
explained, were to be felled and used to construct
a log cabin on the lake shore. As part of the
bargain they asked for permission to use a section
of Dr. Lyman's land that bordered the lake as a
site for their camp.

The plan struck the physician as being capital
and he was particularly pleased to find that the
boys were eager to earn their pleasure with good
hard work. In fact he was so pleased that he
made a bargain whereby the boys would get one
cord of wood in every four cut and they could have
their wood either in trees or in cord wood lengths,
just as they desired. Under this arrangement it

was quite apparent that the boys would have more than enough lumber to build their log cabin and Dr. Lyman told them that he would buy whatever extra wood fell to their share and pay for it at the market price of pulp wood.

Moreover, to help the boys, the physician arranged to have Paul Nez, an experienced timber cruiser, traverse the woods, blazing each tree of the proper pulp wood species and size thus giving the boys a clear idea of what timber to cut and what to leave standing. And Bruce and Jiminy were asked to accompany him so that they might become familiar with the forest.

Tramping the length and breadth of twenty-five acres of wood land, blazing every tree between six and eight inches, was not the easiest sort of work the scouts had ever undertaken, and when they finally arrived at Woodbridge at four o'clock in the afternoon they were "plum tuckered," to quote Jiminy.

However, a brief rest and a hearty evening meal put them in fine shape once more and they were able to get to the troop headquarters betimes that evening, for a meeting had been called at which plans were to be laid for the start of the lumber camp.

Mr. Ford was at headquarters to hear the details of the cruise from Jiminy and Bruce, and he also gave the scouts some expert advice as to the equipment they would want for the beginning of the camp on the morrow.

Among other things he suggested that they build a winter camp immediately by putting up lean-tos with thatched roofs on the shores of the lake. These would be warmer than their tents and would make more or less comfortable quarters until along toward snow time, when the big log cabin the lads hoped to build would be well on its way toward completion. Then, too, these structures could be left in the woods and would always be ready for the boys, whereas if they used their tents they would have to make and break camp every Saturday. The Assistant Scoutmaster also made out lists of provisions, clothes and equipment for the boys and they spent a busy evening getting everything together and in shape for an early start next morning.

In the weird half light of dawn next day, long

before Woodbridge was awake and stirring, nearly a score of scouts were hustling toward headquarters on the crown of Otter Hill. Every lad
was in uniform and most of them wore mackinaws
or sweaters to keep out the early morning chill.

Also each carried the family ax, and over his
shoulder blanket roll and haversack.

"Old Nanc," the troop's automobile, stood in
front of the old machine shop piled high with tar-
paulins, cooking utensils, provisions, and a dozen
and one other things that the scouts used in their
summer camp, and in the driver's seat was Brad
Henshaw, Dr. Lyman's chauffeur. Several of the
boys found room for themselves on the running
board; the others went on their motorcycles, which
were to be brought back in the car, for there was
no safe place in camp for such things.

It was with considerable groaning and grumbling that the home-made automobile finally got
under way, but when she was safely started the
rest of the expedition followed in her wake, and
trundled on toward their destination.

A little after sun-up found the lads at the lake
shore. Here "Old Nanc" and the cycles were

halted, for there was no chance of her making her way along the uneven wood road that skirted the lake for half a mile before it turned and entered the heart of the forest.

At this point the scouts detrained, as it were, and deposited all their luggage on the ground. Then, having unloaded the automobile, they proceeded to reload her, this time with her brood of gasoline-fed ducklings. This done the outfit was turned over to Brad again who immediately started back to Woodbridge.

For an hour after the departure of the automobile the scouts were as busy as bees carrying their paraphernalia to the camp site which they had picked out on the lake shore at the point where the wood road turned and entered the forest. Here was a little stretch of high ground that had been partly cleared by wind-falls and Bruce and Jiminy had selected it as an ideal location for the camp and site for the troop's future log cabin headquarters.

With practically three patrols at work it did not take the lads long to clear away the underbrush and fallen logs in the open space. Indeed

the whack, whack of their hatchets and the heavier
cluck, cluck of their axes could be heard on all
sides of the clearing and in a surprisingly short
time a big space had been made ready for the
camp.   Dozens of young cedars and fir trees were
felled for the lean-tos and in short order the lads
were busy with hammers and nails putting up the
frame-work of six of these shelters.

They worked with a will and the little forest
settlement grew apace.   After the frame work of
the structures was completed the scouts set to
work with clasp knives and hatchets and stripped
the cedars and firs of their branches.   Then with
this material they began to thatch the sides and
roof of the lean-tos working the twigs in and out
until they formed a thickly matted protection
against the weather.   They worked with a will in
spite of cut and blistered fingers and pitch blackened hands until it began to look as if they would
have their little lumbering village finished and
ready for occupancy by mid-afternoon.

At half past eleven Romper Ryan, Ray Martin
and Buster Benson knocked off shelter-building,
for they had been appointed cooks for the camp.

Hastily they put together a big stone fireplace well away from any leaves and underbrush, and after they had a good fire going they began preparing the first meal at the Quarry Scout lumber camp.

The three lads elected to the commissary department were the best cooks in the troop, and they did themselves proud on that particular occasion, for when Romper finally sounded his call to quarters on the bottom of the tin dishpan there were stacks of golden brown country sausages, snowy white boiled potatoes, savory strips of fried bacon, three big pots of steaming hot coffee and last, but not least, nearly a hundred chocolate doughnuts which Jiminy Gordon's mother had contributed just by way of showing the boys how much she thought of them.

In a jiffy seventeen youngsters were assembled in line, tin plate and cup in hand. One by one they filed past the three cooks and received their portions, and shortly after they were all sitting cross legged on the ground, each devoting his full attention to filling a vacant space just under his belt. The only sound that could be heard was the scraping of knives and forks against the tin plates, and now and then a grunt of satisfaction, for their work in the open had given the lads appetites of young sharks.

"Um-m-m, jiminy, that was some feed!" grunted Jiminy Gordon as he put down his plate and wiped his mouth on his handkerchief.

"You said it, only I wish I could have just one more helping of sausages and maybe a little more potatoes; I think I'd feel entirely satisfied then," said fat Babe Wilson, looking pleadingly at Romper.

"Aw give him enough to eat, Romper, he's only had three helpings already," jeered Bud Weir.

"Sorry, Babe, but you've cleaned us out. There isn't a potato or a sausage left," said Romper.

"Gee, that's a fine note. Want to starve him?" said Ray Martin, sarcastically.

"Hi, don't you talk. You got your share before we did. Pretty soft being a cook. I'd like to have that job myself," snorted Babe Wilson.

"You leave Ray alone, Babe. He's some cook, he is. So is Romper, too, only he lets his old fire smoke. Look at that yellow haze up there among the trees. Did your fire make all that smoke, Romper?" said Bruce.

"My fire—why—blame it all it's out. It's plum down to ashes—and, gee! I didn't heat any dish water. Hi, Buster, what did you let that fire go out for? I told you to put some wood on and heat water."

"I—I—aw, I was so hungry I forgot about it. Never mind I'll build it again. I—"

"Say, Romper, is your fire really out?" queried Bruce, looking at the fireplace. Then he added:

"Sure enough, but by gollies I smell some—I hope it isn't—gee, look over to the west there above the trees: Is that smoke? Is it? Say, fellows, can it be a forest fire? Gee, I hope not."

"Forest fire!" exclaimed half a dozen scouts.

Every lad jumped to his feet immediately and looked in the direction Bruce was pointing. And there they beheld a pall of yellow smoke hanging low above the tree tops. They could smell it, too. The pungent odor of burning hemlock was so strong as to be unmistakable. Then for the first time the lads noted that the sunlight seemed dimmed too.

"Jove, I believe it *is* a forest fire," cried Bud Weir.

"I'll bet—say, fellows, look at those big jack rabbits, and there's a fox, and look at the birds. It's a forest fire all right, or those animals wouldn't be running out in the open like that and streaking it for the lake. Cracky what'll we do? I— Hi, Bruce, what's getting you, you're as pale as a ghost?"

Every lad turned toward the leader of the Owl Patrol, who stood as if stricken dumb with horror. But even as they gazed at him he shook off the mental fetters and immediately became a lad of action.

"Fellows," he cried, "listen! There's a man in there—in the fire. Perhaps three of them. Jiminy, you remember, Dave—Dave, what's-his-name—Connors. You know, the fellow in camp over there with the twisted ankle. We saw him yesterday. He's probably in there yet. We must get him out. He can't move, and a forest fire's about the most terrible thing in the world. Quick, fellows! Get your blankets and wet 'em in the lake. Quick, now! Follow me!"

CHAPTER XV

A NARROW ESCAPE

AS usual Dave Connors awoke to find himself alone in camp that morning. Jack and Bart, his camping companions, had left at dawn and gone out partridge hunting exactly as they had done every day since Dave fell down into the gully and twisted his ankle. They were thoughtful enough to leave the coffee pot within reach of Dave's cot, however, along with some fried strips of bacon, bread and butter and a couple of boiled eggs, so that the injured man did not have to hobble about to get his own breakfast.

Dave dashed a cup of water over his hands and splashed a little in his face by way of performing his toilet and then sitting on the edge of his cot, proceeded to devour what was before him eagerly, for, although his foot was injured, his appetite was entirely healthy.

"Um—m—m that was good," he muttered as

he wiped his mouth on his sleeve and looked down at his bandaged foot.

"Now if my old kick was in good order I'd go for a long tramp with a gun but— Ah,—ouch— still sore and swollen. Guess I won't be able to hobble about for a couple of days yet," he reflected as he felt of the injured member.

Then steadying himself on the edge of the cot with the assistance of a cane that Jack cut for him three days before, he hobbled to the tent doorway and looked out.

"Jove, what a corking day! It's a shame I had to get laid up right at the beginning of the trip. But I'll be all right in a couple of days and I suppose I can stand it as long as my books hold out. But, blame it all, look at this camp. Jack and Bart are the sloppiest fellows I ever saw. Look at the blankets on the ground again and the papers scattered everywhere. And look at the big fire they've left. What for, I wonder? I wish I could get out there and clean up the place. I'll speak to them to-night. I don't think such conditions are sanitary. I—I—ouch, blast it, I can't clean up the place," and with a look of disgust the man from Boston limped over to his camp chair and picked up the book that had held his interest the day before.

How long he had been reading he did not know; perhaps an hour, perhaps two. But suddenly he was aroused by a strange, unnatural cracking sound. He looked up with a start, and his eyes dilated with horror at what he saw.

There, not ten feet from him, creeping and writhing through the dried grass and leaves and darting long yellow tongues toward him menacingly, wormed a streak of fire.

It was like a serpent that had crawled out of the embers and sought to catch him unawares. Slowly it moved forward, fanned by the fall breeze until it was a big V extending across the camp clearing, with each arm burning.

On it advanced, licking up everything in its path. Here it consumed a leaf, there a scrap of paper, and each time it devoured something it waxed stronger and more threatening. Even while Dave sat there staring at it, it reached a dried branch. With a crackle this burst into flame, setting fire in turn to a sheet of newspaper nearby. Instantly this was a burning torch. Dave tried to knock it out with his cane. But before he could reach it a gust of wind seized and whirled it across the opening, flinging it spitefully against a fir tree.

With a hiss and a crackling roar this blazed up. In a moment it was a column of fire stretching skyward. The sight was terrible to behold. Then like a whirlwind the arms of fire reached out and enveloped another tree, and sparks flying with the wind lodged in a spruce nearby and converted it into a roaring furnace. And thus in the space of a minute a forest fire was started!

The scorching heat of the burning spruce brought Dave to his senses. He saw before him a hideous fate. Heedless of the pain in his foot he jumped up. His handkerchief he plunged into a pail of drinking water just inside the tent door, then with this wrapped about his face and mouth and with his stout cane in hand, he scrambled across the clearing and into the long wood road that led eastward through the forest toward the lake, half a mile distant.

Oh, if he could run! If he could only have the

use of his injured foot for fifteen minutes, he thought, as he limped on. Behind him he could hear the roar of the fire as it reached out and gathered energy by licking up tree after tree. The air was filled with smoke, pungent and nauseating. All about in the forest on either side of the road livid tongues upleaping, consuming everything and growing stronger every moment.

On hobbled the man from Boston, trying desperately to make time; trying mightily to cheat the fire demons that shrieked and roared behind him. And he was not the only one that was fleeing from the seething furnace that once had been a cool autumn woods. Three deer whisked by him like flashes of the fire itself. Rabbits, skunks and foxes darted here and there among the trees, all headed for the safety of the lake. And a big black bear lumbered by, grunting with every gallop. How Dave envied them. They would be safe. Would he?

Forward he hurried, braving excruciating pain in his injured limb to save his life. Acrid smoke blasts swept down upon him and almost stifled him. On every side he could feel the heat of the

flames. Once a spark dropped upon his shoulder
and fired his shirt. With a cry he beat it out and
strove harder. The pain in his foot was unbearable. It made the perspiration stand out upon his
forehead. It made him whirl with giddiness.
But on he plunged, fighting the fire, the smoke and
the pain and striving his hardest to gain the lake.

Once he thought of Jack and Bart and grew
very bitter, for somehow the fire seemed the result of their carelessness. Would *they* be trapped
by it? They had two good strong legs. They
would save themselves, he hoped. So must he!
Gritting his teeth and stifling a groan, he tried to
gallop, using the cane and injured foot in unison.
It was painful, but he must make time—he must
go fast, faster.

The fire was close behind. It was gaining. He
could hear its triumphant roar. It would catch
him soon. Only a few minutes and a fiery arm
would reach out like a python and wrap about him.
The thought made him shudder.

"No! No! It must not reach me!" he cried
in horror and leapt forward. But his cane slipped
and jammed between his legs. He tripped and

lost his balance. In a mad effort to save himself from falling he put his injured foot forward. His entire weight came down upon it and the ankle snapped. The pain was more than he could stand. With a cry of agony he sank into a limp heap.

Bruce's startling revelation that there was a life to be saved spurred the scouts to action. One more glance in the direction of the smoke pall to the westward and in a twinkle every lad had his blanket in hand and was sousing it into the lake. Handkerchiefs were doused too, for the youngsters knew well that the smoke would soon be so thick that they would need this kind of protection.

And while the rest were thus occupied, Bruce held a hasty conference with Jiminy, and the two boys quickly cut scout staffs. With these in hand they waved the troop forward and started off at a mad pace up the wood road to meet the advancing forest fire.

On they raced, the smoke growing heavier and more pungent as they neared the flames. They could hear the deep toned muttering of the conflagration. And all the way along the road they were breasting a tide of forest dwellers, deer, rabbit, bears, and a host of smaller animals, all scurring away from the roaring doom behind them.

Soon the lads were in the zone of flying sparks. Here and there along the road small fires were being started. These were quickly beaten out, for the boys were determined not to have their retreat cut off. As they moved forward Bruce's heart grew heavy, for he could see that already the flames had swept by the camping site of Dave Connors and his companions. The patrol leader hoped fervently that the injured youth had been able to keep ahead of the rushing fire.

They were approaching the fire belt. Their eyes smarted from the smoke. They could feel the heat on every hand. They pulled their hats low to protect their foreheads and pushed on. Fire was everywhere. Here and there pine trees burst into flames with a hiss and a roar, and now and then blazing branches would come hurling through space to fall with a crash in the roadway.

Bruce began to be worried. Had he brought

the scouts out on a dangerous but useless mission? Had Dave Connors come down the wood road, or had he gone wandering blindly through the forest to be trapped and burned to death? Perhaps even now he was a charred mass somewhere back there in that seething forest. The smoke was so thick that the boys could not see two feet ahead of them, but they struggled forward, beating out menacing tongues of flames on every hand, hoping to keep the roadway open for a retreat.

Through the smoke they groped; bending low and breathing through their wet handkerchiefs. Their eyes burned. Their lungs pained with the gases they had inhaled, but they pushed on until suddenly with a cry Bruce stumbled and pitched forward.

But he was on his feet in an instant, and examining the apparently lifeless mass in the roadway that had tripped him. Then with a shout of delight, he summoned Jiminy and in an instant a coat stretcher was made with the aid of the scout staffs they had cut. Then with the limp form of Dave Connors between them the two scouts started struggling back toward the lake. Away from the fire they raced with the troop behind them still beating out the menacing sparks and flames.

Forward they hurried, but as they advanced this time their way grew easier and the smoke less pungent. Soon they were among the refugees again. Rabbits, mink and foxes scuttled along with them, and the boys had to turn out to keep from treading on some of the smaller animals who could not travel as fast as their bigger woods neighbors. The heat of the fire was left behind and falling sparks no longer bothered them. Their way to the lake was clear.

A few minutes later they reached the knoll upon which their lumber camp was being constructed. Here they paused long enough to permit Bruce and Jiminy to administer first aid to the unconscious Dave Connors. And while the lads were reviving him, others gathered together hatchets, axes, cooking utensils and whatever else they could conveniently carry, and bidding farewell to their doomed camp they made ready for a plunge into the shallows of the lake.

All that afternoon and a good part of the evening, the scouts stood shoulder deep in the cool waters and watched the landscape burn. Acres and acres of woodland with thousands of dollars' worth of timber was consumed before their eyes. Dave watched it sadly, for he knew that all this ruin had been wrought by him and his careless camping companions.

Every shallow of the lake was crowded with animal life of all kinds, and the lads knew that thousands of forest dwellers must have perished in that inferno. They stood among deer and bears and other more timid forest dwellers, but the fear of man and the natural enmity toward each other was completely blotted out by the greater fear of the fire, and a seeming sense of comradeship born of common danger.

Night came, and the sky was a livid pink. The lake had checked the fire's advance to the eastward and the wind had driven the flames north toward the mountains. Further and further away traveled the flames painting the sky a sinister color and producing a spectacle that the scouts never forgot.

At midnight, though the woods still smoldered, the boys contemplated leaving the shallows in which they had been standing and going ashore, for they argued that if the heat from the embers was not too intense they could work along the margin of the lake until they reached the opposite shore.

But while they were contemplating this, off across the lake they saw lights advancing toward them. They heard shouts, too, and they shouted in answer, and it was not long before they had guided a flotilla of small boats toward them. This proved to be a rescuing party organized and headed by the anxious Mr. Ford and old Dr. Lyman, who were almost distracted until they made doubly certain that every lad was safe and whole of limb and body.

CHAPTER XVI

"WHEW-W-W! Hi, shut that door—good night! want to freeze us out?" shouted Romper Ryan, as he glared across the workshop at Bruce Clifford and Bud Weir.

"Aw, don't get fidgety. You won't ever freeze the way you're hanging over that forge. What's the matter, Romper?" asked Bruce.

"Busted the frame of my snowshoe. Trying to make a little brace for it and get it fixed up before you fellows arrived."

"When'll you be ready? Where are the rest of the fellows?"

"They're upstairs. I'll be ready in a jiffy now."

The two scouts crossed the shop and made their way noisily up the wooden stairs to the meeting room, where they found half a dozen lads in an animated discussion as to where the biggest and best Christmas trees were to be found.

"I tell you the forest fire cleaned everything out of the Long Lake district," asserted Ray Martin.

"Well, I suppose you want us to go all the way over into Bland County this cold day," said fat Babe Wilson sarcastically.

"Speaking of forest fires," said Bruce, who had come into the room just in time to hear Ray Martin's remark; "speaking of forest fires, did any of you fellows see the Northern Lights last night up back of Haystack Mountain? Father and I thought first it was a forest fire. The sky was all pink and white. But we concluded it must have been the reflection of the Aurora Borealis. You can see 'em this time of year, you know. Snow helps their reflection, Pop says."

"Is that what it was? I saw it too, and when I saw the red glow in the sky I just naturally thought of that Long Lake fire last month. Say, by the way I got a postal card from that fellow in Boston, we rescued. Remember? Dave Connors is his name— Gollies, every time I think of forest fires I shudder.   He sure had a close squeek and so did we.   That's why that glow in the sky last night sort of made an impression on me.   I wondered if any one was caught in it, same as we were nearly caught?" said Nipper Knapp.

"Aw, I tell you it wasn't a fire.   It was the Northern Lights back of Haystack Mountain. Dad said so, and he knows, and, say, speaking of Haystack Mountain," added Bruce, "why not go up there for our tree?   If this is going to be the town's Christmas tree it must be a whopper. Most all of that land up there belongs to the people Mr. Ford works for and he has permission from them to cut as many trees as we need.   How about it?"

"By jiminy! that's just what I said, Bruce," cried Jiminy Gordon, "and Romper agrees with me."

"Sure I do," said Romper, suddenly making his appearance from the workshop, his mended snow-shoe in hand.

"Then it's Haystack Mountain.   Come on, fel-lows, get ready; half the morning will be gone before we start," said Bruce, and in a twinkle a half-score of scouts were donning mackinaws and sweaters and making themselves generally secure against a temperature that hovered very close to the zero mark. And five minutes later the entire crew, armed with axes and snowshoe-shod were to be seen leaving headquarters in single file and heading up Otter Creek Valley over three feet of December snow.

Woodbridge had once more honored the Quarry Troop. But the lads had earned the honor by suggesting that the town hold a public celebration in the square in front of the Town Hall on Christmas Eve. Moreover, they had worked their hardest to gain the interest of village officials, ministers, and men and women of the community in such a celebration and it could well be said that through the efforts of the khaki-clad youngsters, Woodbridge, as a community, would for the first time welcome the coming of Christmas. Neighbors and friends, rich and poor, young and old, would stand shoulder to shoulder this Christmas Eve and sing the joy and happiness of the Yuletide.

And for their share in the organization work

the scouts had been granted the privilege of providing the town with a big community Christmas tree, which was to stand in the center of the square and be decorated from bottom to tip with colored electric lights. This decorating was an affair of the Quarry Scouts also. They had been given the commission by Mayor Worthington and the councilmen to do all the electric wiring and the stringing of the bulbs.

Of course the lads welcomed such an important task, for they were eager to demonstrate how useful they could be. Also they were pleased to display their knowledge of mechanics. So it can be easily understood why Bruce and his chums were eager to get an early start the Saturday morning a week before Christmas. They intended to search the woods for the tallest and straightest fir tree in the township.

In spite of the fact that their ears tingled with the bitter cold and the wind whistled through the valley, whirling the powdery crystals of snow into their faces, the scouts were a happy lot of youngsters as they swung their way northward. Who could be other than happy with Christmas but a

week off? Snowballs flew thick and fast among
them, and now and then snowshoe races were run,
too.

The lads chose the valley bottom for their journey and avoided the highway which swung to the
left and made a wide detour before the byroad
that approached Haystack Mountain joined it.
With this route the lads could cut down the journey at least three miles and then, too, they had
fine snow for shoeing.

Soon they had left the open and entered the
hardwood belt from which all the firs and other
evergreens had long since been trimmed. Snow-
shoeing through the woods was not so much of a
lark, for the lads had no trail to follow and must
needs work their way between half-covered underbrush. The snow was softer here, too, and their
shoes dragged. But most of their surplus energy
had been worked off by this time and they were
willing to settle down to single file. Each took his
turn breaking a trail.

On they traveled for more than an hour, always
keeping the shoulder of Haystack Mountain, which
loomed up above the tree line, their objective.

About half a mile from the mountain they suddenly came clear of the woods and into the highway. Here a brief conference was held as to the
advisability of trying to climb the shoulder of
the mountain or taking the road which led around.
The last route was decided upon, because up here
the thoroughfare was little traveled and was practically unbroken. Indeed, they saw signs of very
few sleighs having passed there since the snowstorm four days previous.

Away they swung, keeping an eye out on either
side of the road for a Christmas tree, but they
did not find a fir tall enough to be used for the
town's tree.

Soon they were around the shoulder of the
mountain and traveling west. The woods were
thicker here and trees more numerous. But there
was a peculiar odor of burnt wood in the air, too,
which all the scouts detected.

"Cracky! I believe your Northern Light *was* a
forest fire, or—or—say, isn't that smoke rising
above those trees there?" demanded Nipper
Knapp.

"Right, by gollies!" shouted Bruce, "but—oh,

I know, now. There's a little farm in there. It's been vacant for—no, it hasn't, by jingoes! an old lady has been living there all Fall. I've seen her in town. Nanny Haskells, they call her. Cracky! come on, fellows, maybe the poor old soul has been burned to death!"

The scouts were off at a gallop, stirring up the snow like a whirlwind as they loped along the road. Soon they came to an unbroken lane through the woods. Into this they turned and a hundred yards further on they emerged into the little farm clearing. What a sight met their eyes.

In a smoldering, smoking heap of charred ruins lay what remained of an old-fashioned farmhouse and barn that had stood there for years. The fire had burned itself out, except here and there where glowing coals showed themselves. Only two blackened timbers remained standing. And in this picture of devastation, looking the most lonesome and pathetic figure in the world, wandered the tiniest, most old-fashioned and motherly looking woman the lads had ever seen.

She seemed all but distracted with her misery,

for she went about wringing her hands and sobbing as if her heart were broken. Here and there
she picked her way, peering into the smoking
ashes and now and then poking among them for
a trinket or a keepsake that the fire had only
blackened. It was a pathetic sight indeed, and
the sturdy scouts all felt heavy hearted as they
watched her.

Finally Bruce left the group and went toward
her. Then for the first time the little woman
looked up, startled at first. But when she saw
the uniforms the lads wore she was no longer
frightened. In truth, she seemed to welcome them
as the only sympathetic human beings she had seen
to whom she could tell her woes.

"Oh, boys, boys, it's gone, all, all gone. Look
—my old home all in ruins. Oh, dear! oh, dear!
I'm so miserable. What shall I ever do? Why
should this be taken from me, too? They took—
they took her—her—and, oh, dear! oh, dear! what
shall I do?" she cried.

Bruce put his hands out to comfort her as best
he could and the little lady came toward him and
laid her head upon his chest, sobbing as if her

heart was broken. But the all-night strain on one so old had been too great and presently she became very quiet, so quiet indeed that Bruce became frightened and looked down into her face. And instantly he realized that she was completely worn out.

"Here, fellows," he called in a business-like tone, "the poor old lady is all in. We must take her to town and get her into the hospital. Come, fellows, quickly now. You, Jiminy, and Nipper, make a coat stretcher—cut some staffs—strong ones. The three of us will take her back to town. The rest of you fellows go after the Christmas tree. But first lend us a jacket or a sweater or two to bundle the old lady in."

In a twinkle the scouts were busy. Staffs were cut, the stretcher constructed and old Nanny made comfortable with extra coats and sweaters that the more warmly clad scouts could spare. Then, as the three lads started townward, Bruce shouted:

"Hi, Bud, see that you get a whopping big tree. A thirty footer, if you can. We'll be back in an hour or so to help you. So long."

Crisp weather and an additional snowstorm

during the week that preceded the holidays gave the youngsters of the Vermont town full assurance of a white Christmas. And they would have been mightily disappointed lads if such had not been the case, for what would a Community Christmas celebration and a town Christmas tree be like without snow everywhere? It was good packing snow, too, as numerous snow fights at noon time, on the academy campus, attested.

But, aside from these noon-day diversions, the Quarry Scouts had little time to indulge in Winter sports that week. The hills about town were just right for coasting and the broad Champlain Valley stretched north and south to be explored on snowshoes, skis, and with sleigh-riding parties, but the scouts could not find time to enjoy these opportunities. Rather, they found their fun in anticipating a good time after Christmas, providing the snow lasted, for they had work to do. There was the big Christmas tree to be erected and trimmed.

It was a monster tree. Thirty-two feet from base to tip, and as it lay there in front of the town hall waiting to be elevated into position, it commanded the admiration of the whole town. Thursday afternoon, after the carpenters had finished a big platform and grandstand, the lads erected timber shears and block and tackle and set the tree into place in the very center of the pavilion, which was to accommodate the mayor, town officials, visitors, the orchestra and a host of school children who were to sing carols.

" Wow, it looks great," said Nipper Knapp, surveying the tall fir proudly, "and won't it look corking after we get it all trimmed to-morrow afternoon?"

"Yes, but mind you, fellows, we'll have to work like everything to-morrow. All the wiring has to be strung and all the lights put on between one o'clock in the afternoon and half past four. It'll be some job," said Bud Weir.

"You're right it will," said Bruce, "thank goodness we have everything shipshape up at headquarters to get a good start. There's more than enough wire in the lot Mr. Ford sent over. And I guess we must have put on about three thousand lamp sockets during the last few days, haven't we?"

"Two thousand and eighty-seven," corrected Romper, "and it's a good thing school lets out at noon to-morrow."

"It'll be a sight for sore eyes. Say, fellows, I'll tell you what. Let's bring old Nanny Haskell down and give her a seat on the visitors' stand. I guess Mr. Ford could arrange that for us. It might cheer the poor old soul up a little. How is she to-day? Any one been up to the hospital?"

"Sure, Romper and I were up there. She's all well and ready to leave, but the poor thing hasn't any place to go to, it seems. She's bluer than all git out, too. Jiminy, but I feel sorry for her," said Jiminy Gordon.

"Well, then, by gollies! we'll see if we can't make her happy on Christmas Eve at least. We'll have her all bundled up and bring her down here. Listening to the kids sing and all the fun and things might help her spirit a little."

"Fine idea, if she'll come," said Bruce.

"Oh, we'll arrange that, all right, I think," replied Romper. "I'll go up to the hospital to-morrow. Perhaps Mr. Ford will go along, and we can talk it over with Doctor Bassett."

"Good enough; I'll go with you. And now let's go home and get some supper, fellows. It's getting dark," said Bruce. And presently the scouts were tramping off through the snowy Winter twilight to their respective homes.

Fortunately, Mr. Clifford allowed Bruce the use of Blossom, his big black trotting horse, and a light box sleigh, or otherwise the lads would have had to make a dozen trips up the steep, snow-covered Otter Hill to headquarters to get their coils of wire and boxes of lamps to town next day.

As it was, the spirited animal had to haul three sleigh-loads of equipment to the Town Hall before the scouts could even start the task of decorating. As soon as the coils of wire arrived a dozen scouts began to swarm the big Christmas tree, looping the wires from branch to branch and fastening them securely. Other scouts followed in their wake and screwed red, white and blue, green and yellow lamps into the vacant sockets. And while all this was going on, a crew of linemen and meter-setters from the local electric light company were running an extension, or service line, from the nearest street wires, for the electric company had promised to furnish current free for the evening's celebration.

The square was a very busy place for several hours that afternoon, and every one was working with a will for he realized that he must be finished before dusk came. By half past three, however, the scouts found that they could ease up a little for, with the arrival of one more load of colored lamps from headquarters, the tree would be thoroughly decorated even to the shining electrically illuminated star on top which Jiminy Gordon placed there with the help of an extra long ladder.

"Whoope-e-e! almost through. Don't it look fine, eh? And here comes Bruce with the last load of lamps. Come on, fellows, and help unload the sleigh," shouted Bud Weir as Jiminy finally reached the ground after he had finished wiring the big star in place.

"Right-o-o! and last man to the curb is no good," shouted Nipper Knapp, starting to run. Next moment there was a scurry of scouts through the snow that covered the square and a pell-mell race to the curb where Bruce drew up the panting Blossom with a jingle of bells and a shower of powdery snow.

"Whoa there, Blossom," he shouted. Then to the scouts, "Come on, you duffers, and get these things unloaded. I want to get the horse into the stable so I can do some work, too."

The "duffers" arrived with a rush and in a twinkle the boxes were being removed from the sleigh in a manner quite violent, and this to the imminent peril of the contents.

"Hi, not so bloomin' reckless," shouted Bruce, "don't smash 'em, whatever you do. They are the last colored lamps in town and we need 'em. And, say—listen—what's the fuss up the street? Hear 'em shoutin'? Gee, it's a runaway an' here it comes—no—no—it's going to turn down High Street toward the railroad—an'—cracky! fellows, there's a freight pulling out of the siding! See the smoke! And there's a woman and a girl in the cutter! Wow! Look at those chumps up the street shoutin' and wavin' their arms. That's no way to stop a horse! Those women will be killed. Hi, Bud, hop in here. Come on, we've got to stop 'em. I'm goin' after 'em with Blossom. Gee*tyap* there, Blossom. Git, now, that's t' girl. Go!"

There could be no mistaking the fact that the horse and cutter coming down the street was a runaway. The big animal was almost mad with fright. His eyes bulged out until the whites showed and its nostrils were distended with fear. And, to make matters worse, there were a dozen men and boys shouting and waving their hands in a foolish effort to stop the horse. But all that they accomplished was to make the animal still more frightened.

Fortunately, Bud's mind acted as quickly as Bruce's. He came into the sleigh with a bound, but almost before he landed Bruce had Blossom under way. Just a touch of the whip was all that was needed and the nervous trotter shot forward like a flash of lightning. A moment later she was a jet black streak flying toward the corner of High Street around which the runaway cutter had just disappeared.

Almost in the wink of an eye Blossom reached the corner and swept around it at a gallop while the sleigh careened first on one runner and then upon the other, each time on the brink of turning over and pitching its occupants into the snow-banks that lined the road. But the scouts gave no heed to this. All their attention was on the flying cutter a hundred yards ahead and upon the railroad crossing half a mile down the road. The freight train had left the siding, and at the moment the scouts rounded the corner she was chugging her way slowly toward the crossing. Of course, the gates were down but this only added to the peril. The runaway horse was blind with fright. He would plunge into the gates, tear through them and probably kill himself and the women in the sleigh by dashing headlong into the freight train.

"Go it, Bruce, go it. We *must* save them. They'll be killed if we don't," cried the half frantic Bud.

And Bruce, pale of face but determined, cut Blossom with the whip to urge her forward. Rarely was the trotter treated that way and when the cut came she leapt forward like a deer. Then her racing instinct seemed to come back to her. She knew what was wanted. The horse ahead must be passed. She stretched her long legs to their utmost and the pace she set made the light sleigh pitch and rock like a ship in a gale. Bruce never used the whip again. Indeed, he tossed it into the road, for he must needs use two hands to govern the flying horse.

The animal ahead was flying, too, and it was a question for a few moments whether the scouts could make up the distance. But Blossom was at her best. Faster and faster she went while town folk stood on the sidewalk and gaped in amazement at the pace she held. The hundred-yard lead was cut down to fifty, now to forty, thirty-five, thirty. Bruce and Bud could see the look of terror on the faces of the girl and the woman in the cutter. Also they could see the reason for the accident. The reins had parted and one short length dangled over the horse's side and slapped him continually on the ribs while the longer section dragged under the cutter.

"We'll make it, Bud, we'll make it. We've *got* to make it. I'll drive like mad. We'll start to pass them and I'll run Blossom as close as I dare and then when we get abreast of the horse you hang out upon the running-board, and jump for the shafts of the cutter. Get astride the horse's back and grab those reins. Get ready, Bud! Out on the running-board, now! Hurry!" cried Bruce.

Blossom was drawing abreast of the cutter. Bud clung to the running-board and crouched for a spring.

"Go it, Blossom," cried Bruce. "Good old girl, go it. Go on, go on. Get ready, Bud—steady— ready now—*jump!*"

Bud reached far out and leaped. One foot struck the shafts. He threw himself forward and grasped the runaway's mane and in an instant he had swung himself astride the horse's back. For a moment all that he could do was cling to the swaying animal. And when the horse felt the extra weight drop upon him he bounded forward like a stag. uttering a shrill whinny of fear.

For a fleeting moment the lad thought of the peril of his position. But when he recalled that the lives of two women depended upon him, he became active. Reaching forward he grasped the broken line and the long one and forced the bit home into the horse's mouth. The animal snorted and plunged. Bud pulled back again. The runaway reared and pawed the air, snorting and shaking its massive head. "Whoa," cried the scout, "whoa, boy, steady now," and it seemed as if the animal recognized the authority in his command for the next time the lad reined in the panic-stricken horse slowed up and presently came to a complete standstill and stood trembling like a leaf.

Then, when the scout looked up for the first time, there, not twenty yards away, was the railroad crossing, with the freight train rumbling slowly by.

"Fine work, Bud, fine," cried Bruce, who had pulled in on Blossom the moment the scout had jumped from the sleigh. "Fine work, and—and —gee! but it was a narrow escape."

Indeed it had been a narrow escape. Bud realized it as well as Bruce. And so did the woman and the little girl in the cutter, for their faces were white and they hardly had strength enough left to step from the cutter when Bruce tried to assist them.

"Goodness me, what a day—what a day," said

the woman, trembling with nervousness. And when the little girl heard this she began to cry.

"Oh, mother, I'm unhappy, too," she wept. "Poor Nanny, poor Nanny, just think she's been burned to death, and all because you and father sent me to school last September. Oh, mother, mother, it's terrible. And then the horse acting up like that. I—I—oh, Mr.—er—Mr. Boy Scout, do you know anything about old Nanny—Nanny Haskell? She was my dear nurse. Last Fall she left our house in St. Cloud because my father and mother sent me to school down in Boston. She— she—oh, dear!—she said she wouldn't live in St. Cloud without me, because she would be too lonesome, so she came back to her old farm in the woods here, where she hadn't been for ten years, and—now—oh, dear! oh, dear;—it burned down— and—Nanny must have been burned to death."

"Why—why—no—no, she wasn't burned to death," said Bruce, when he fully understood, "she—she—why she's over in the Woodbridge hospital. That big building over there on Willow Street. We found her and took her there, and she wasn't a bit hurt, only sick, that's all."

"What! is she alive—really—honest—Nanny Haskell—boy, you're sure?" cried the woman excitedly. "We—we—came over to-day to get her and bring her back to St. Cloud. We wanted to tell her that Genevieve had come home from Boston to stay, and that we wanted her to come back with us on Christmas Eve and live with us for good. Are you sure—?"

"Yes, yes, I'm sure. I helped bring her into town," said Bruce.

"Then come, mother, come. I must see old Nanny and cheer her up. The boys will take care of the horse and put him in a stable. Won't you, boys?" said Genevieve, excitedly.

"Sure—Bud will fix the reins and drive him to the hotel stable. Come into my sleigh and I'll take you to the hospital," said Bruce.

A cold wind was driving powdery flakes out of the darkness overhead when the Woodbridge town folk began to gather in the square to celebrate their first community Christmas. The scouts were there early, for, besides the fact that several of them had the task of taking care of the electric switches that controlled the lights on the big tree, the rest of the troop had been delegated to police the square.

The ceremonies were supposed to begin at eight o'clock, but by half-past seven the big platform was filled with visitors, officials and prominent townsmen. The orchestra had arrived, too, and taken its place, and the chorus of four hundred school children stood waiting, song books in hand. The big square was literally jammed by joyous men and women and shivering, though none the less enthusiastic, youngsters. And over these thousand or more silence reigned and every eye was fastened on the tall somber looking tree.

Then came the signal from the Mayor. The next moment the orchestra leader swung his baton and the orchestra rang forth. Simultaneously the voices of the children took up the opening bars of a good old English Christmas carol. This was the cue the four scouts at the switches were waiting for. One by one they jammed the tiny rubber covered connections home and in circuits of eight and twelve, the colored lamps on the

great tree began to twinkle until it was a blaze
of glory from the lowermost branches to the great
glittering star on the top.

What a wave of applause greeted this illumina-
tion. Then some one in the throng took up the
carol the children were singing and in a moment
thousands of throats were pouring forth the happiness of Yuletide. The people's enthusiasm
seemed boundless.

But though the lights of the great tree revealed
joyous countenances everywhere, the scouts could
single out three in the group on the platform that
seemed far happier than the rest. In truth, tears
of joy were coursing down old Nanny Haskell's
cheeks as she sat there hugging the form of Genevieve to her and listening to the rejoicing of the
vast throng. And close beside them, her arm
about the old nurse's shoulder, sat a very happy
mother.

All through the ceremonies they stayed, lingering even till the lights on the big tree began to go
out in groups. And when the star on the top,
after a preliminary wink, went dark too, they
turned and made their way slowly across the

square to where their cutter, a hired driver in the seat, stood waiting.

"Well, fellows," said Bruce, as with a jingle of bells the sleigh started in the direction of St. Cloud City, "I guess old Nanny's Christmas won't be such a sad one after all, thanks to Bud, here."

And then with boisterous shouts of "Merry Christmas, everybody," the scouts all started for home.

THE END

THE BOY SCOUT LIFE SERIES

Published with the approval of

The Boy Scouts of America

In the boys' world of story books, none better than those about boy scouts arrest and grip attention. In a most alluring way, the stories in the BOY SCOUT LIFE SERIES tell of the glorious good times and wonderful adventures of boy scouts.

All the books were written by authors possessed of an intimate knowledge of this greatest of all movements organized for the welfare of boys, and are published with the approval of the National Headquarters of the Boy Scouts of America.

The Chief Scout Librarian, Mr. F. K. Mathiews, writes concerning them: "It is a bully bunch of books. I hope you will sell 100,000 copies of each one, for these stories are the sort that will help instead of hurt our movement."

THE BOY SCOUT FIRE FIGHTERS—CRUMP

THE BOY SCOUTS OF THE LIGHTHOUSE TROOP—McCLANE

THE BOY SCOUT TRAIL BLAZERS—CHELEY

THE BOY SCOUT TREASURE HUNTERS—LERRIGO

BOY SCOUTS AFLOAT—WALDEN

BOY SCOUTS COURAGEOUS—MATHIEWS

BOY SCOUTS TO THE RESCUE—LERRIGO

BOY SCOUTS ON THE TRAIL—GARTH

THE BOY SCOUTS IN AFRICA—CORCORAN

THE BOY SCOUTS OF ROUND TABLE PATROL—LERRIGO

Publishers
BARSE & CO.

New York, N. Y. Newark, N. J.

THE AVIATION SERIES

By

JOHN PRENTICE LANGLEY

Cloth. 12 mo., Illustrated.

THERE is no other topic of such world-wide interest as Aviation. And that interest will be increased with proposed flights to the South Pole, Japan, and 'Round the World.

"The Aviation Series" by John Prentice Langley, an authority on flying, has been written to further the interest in flying and to tell "Young America", in its own words, the fun, hardships, triumphs and thrills connected with this sport.

In this series you will become acquainted with Amos Green and his friend Dan, two of the most daring young Americans you have ever read about.

1. TRAIL BLAZERS OF THE SKIES.
2. SPANNING THE PACIFIC.
3. MASTERS OF THE AIR-LANES.
4. THE PATHFINDER'S GREAT FLIGHT.
5. AIR VOYAGERS OF THE ARCTIC.
6. DESERT HAWKS ON THE WING.
7. CHASING THE SETTING SUN.
8. BRIDGING THE SEVEN SEAS.

Publishers
BARSE & CO.

New York, N. Y.   Newark, N. J.